# Red Tape

# Michele Lynn Seigfried

Cover Design by LLPix Photography, www.llpix.com
Edited by Hercules Editing and Consulting,
www.bzhercules.com

Visit the author's website at
www.facebook.com/MicheleLynnSeigfried

ISBN-13: 978-1482012880
ISBN-10: 148201288X

First Edition

# DEDICATION

This book is dedicated to my beautiful daughter.
I will love you with all my heart and soul forever.

# A Special Thank You to:

My husband, Mickey for his encouragement.
Author Beth Rinyu for inspiring me to write a novel.
My advance copy readers, Joanne Kruplo & Debbie Bauer.
Municipal Clerk Kathy Norcia for many creative writing ideas.

# 1

*H*e had crazy eyes. That was the first thing I remember about "him." It was in a text message from my assistant, last March: *Oh, my god Chelsey, we have this new guy coming to our meetings. He's nuts. He has crazy eyes.*

Little did I know that Mr. Crazy Eyes was soon to make my life a living hell. I was out on maternity leave, having given birth last month to a beautiful blonde-haired, blue-eyed baby girl named Amanda, "Mandy" for short. Bonnie was my assistant or deputy town clerk, to be exact. She was filling in for me during my absence and she was required to attend the meetings of the town council in my place.

Since I had been home since a month before I went into labor, I was starved for the office gossip, so I quickly responded to her: *Call me!*

Bonnie gave me the scoop. "He" was Robert Triggers. He was unhappy about the lack of dunes at the end of the street where he lived. The owner of the land at the end of the street, Bill Bradford, did not want dunes in front of his house. Bill said the dunes would block the view and diminish his home's value. I had met Bill once when he came to my office to submit his landlord registration form. He seemed like a really nice guy. His property was a rental and I had to guess that he was happy that he didn't have to deal with an irate neighbor most of the time.

Bonnie told me that Triggers was retired from some sort of biotech job and had a lot of free time on his hands. She said he was a large man, over six feet tall and likely pushing three hundred pounds. She called him an eccentric dresser, stating his clothing was often mismatched and his neckties were unusual. He was balding with gray on the sides. His skin was tan and his nose was big. His eyebrows were jet black and overly bushy. She described his eyes as being so dark and cold, that it sent shivers down her spine to look at him.

The mayor, the members of the town council, the attorney, and various others had told him it wasn't possible to install dunes on someone's private property, but this only made Mr. Triggers angrier. He showed up to every meeting, demanding that the town install the dunes.

"He's like a broken record," Bonnie said. "He says, 'Where are my dunes? Where are my dunes? Why all the red tape? Why all the red tape?' I'm having trouble dealing with him."

"What else is going on there?" I asked Bonnie.

"Well, the courtroom caught on fire yesterday."

"Oh my god! Is everyone okay?"

Three court clerks were having dinner in the downstairs kitchen before the night court session. One of the clerks went back to the office to make a phone call. She saw the smoke and picked up the phone to dial 9-1-1, but the phones wouldn't work. The fire alarms did not sound. She left the building and ran across the parking lot to the police headquarters to get help. An officer came back and extinguished the flames that had ignited in a garbage can before the fire trucks arrived. Smoke filled the building and the few people inside had to evacuate.

"Everyone was fine and there is only damage to the courtroom, not any of the offices," Bonnie reported. She told me she missed me and said she didn't know how she was going to handle the next three months without me.

"You're exaggerating. You'll be fine. Call me if you need me."

With that, we said our good-byes.

The Town of Sunshine is a small town—eight square miles and slightly more than four thousand in population. The population swells over the summertime to approximately ten thousand people with part-time residents and tourists. It's located on a barrier island in New Jersey. The bay is on the west; the ocean is on the east. It's incredibly beautiful here. Unique, majestic, mini-mansions sit along the beachfront in an array of pastel colors. Side streets are lined with the cutest bungalows and capes. There are no lawns to mow—residents prefer the convenience of hardscaping at their vacation homes. There is indeed something about this town that is calm and relaxing. The sun, sand, salt air, and sailboats reminded me of a watercolor painting.

It was Friday, March 9th. The baby was still asleep, so I pulled on my slippers and robe and shuffled down the hall to the kitchen to brew some coffee. I chose a Carmel Vanilla

Cream K-cup and made it a latte with my fat-free creamer. I stepped outside to get the newspaper. It felt like spring for the first time this season. I took a deep breath and enjoyed a peaceful moment in the warm sunshine and crisp breeze. The birds were chirping and puffy white clouds passed on by. I hurried back into the house so I could hear Mandy if she stirred. I sat at my breakfast bar and opened the newspaper to see an article on page two. *"Arson in Sunshine Being Investigated."*

*Hmm, Bonnie didn't mention it was arson*, I thought. I read further down the page. "Phone lines and the town's fire alarms were found to be tampered with." I wondered who could do such a thing. A disgruntled ex-employee? An angry taxpayer? A lunatic on the loose? Mr. "Crazy Eyes?" Oh well, there was no time to think about work, the baby was crying and it was time for me to get to diaper and bottle duty.

Looking at my beautiful daughter brought back cherished memories of my childhood. When I was a little girl, my family would rent a cottage on Thirteenth Street in Sunshine during the summer months. I remember running around on the beach in my blonde pigtails. My cousins and I would throw blobs of dead jellyfish at each other and ride the waves on our boogie boards. We would walk back and forth to the beach barefoot for fear of being called "shoobies" by the locals. My fondest memories were here: Grandpop taking us out on his boat for a ride, riding the rollercoaster at the small amusement park down the road, playing games in the arcade, and eating homemade ice cream at the shop at the end of our street. When I was older, I learned how to sail and surf in Sunshine with my cousins.

When I was about sixteen, my grandparents bought that cottage on Thirteenth Street. They gave it an update with new kitchen appliances, bathroom floors, and carpeting. A couple of years later, they added a second floor with two bedrooms and an extra bathroom.

Sadly, they passed away only five years later. The house was left to my parents in their will. At first, we would spend weekends and a couple of weeks at the cottage a year. After my father retired, my parents decided to sell their house and move into the cottage full-time. I mostly remember it seeming like a hotel to me during this period in my life—having only time to sleep and shower there. I was a recent college grad and held down two jobs in order to pay my student loans and to save up for a new car. I would spend weekends on the beach or meeting up with friends at the local pub.

I received a job offer as a Deputy Township Clerk for a township in Middlesex County when I was twenty-four. It paid well enough to allow me to quit my second job. I found an apartment close to work and I bought that new car—a Honda Accord in Alabaster Silver Metallic. It was my first time living away from the shore and my parents. It was the first time I truly felt like an adult.

I met Mandy's father when I was twenty-six, and my interests slowly morphed from having a drink at a bar with friends to settling down and having children. Randy was charming and fun. We had a lot in common and hit it off immediately. At the time, I thought he was my soul mate.

When I was twenty-eight, my Great Uncle Lou passed away. Uncle Lou owned a small home on a lagoon beyond the causeway in a town named Madisen. I remember fondly how my dad would take me to go crabbing off his dock when I was a little girl. Uncle Lou would boil up the crabs and season them with Old Bay. He always served a pasta dish on the side since we never really caught enough to make a decent meal.

I was surprised to learn that Uncle Lou had left his home to me, but I guess since he didn't have any children of his own and since I was the only one of his nieces and nephews that visited him, it made sense. My ex moved in a year later when we got engaged.

My former fiancé and I had a surprise with the pregnancy and we fought constantly during those long months. What should have been a blissful time in my life was stressful and lonely. Randy seemed to want nothing to do with me any longer. We never went out and I went to all my doctor's appointments alone. Randy moved out when the baby arrived. I guess he couldn't take the pressure of giving up his beer guzzling buddies and raising a child.

I was in denial for a while. I thought he would come to his senses and want to be a father once he got over his fears. I thought he would fill the shoes of the man I wanted him to be. No matter how much I wanted him to grow up, at some point I realized I couldn't wish his immaturity away. I also knew I could handle being a single mom. I had recently turned thirty, had a good job and people in my life who were willing to help me. So I let him go and never looked back.

• • •

A couple of weeks passed and I realized I hadn't heard or read any more gossip about Sunshine. I surmised that Mr. Triggers had made himself scarce, leaving Bonnie with little to report. I was thrilled it was finally April. It meant that I would be permitted to drive again after my emergency c-section. I couldn't believe my little one was already two months old. She seemed to be growing like a weed. I knew I shouldn't take her out in public until she had her shots at three months old, but it was hard sitting at home all the time when I was dying to take her out and show her off to everyone. She was such a cutie pie! Since her dad packed his bags, it was only her and me most days. That jerk didn't know what he was missing. My parents, Tom and Mary Alton, came by a few times every week to bring me food and to drive me crazy for a while.

I glanced at my phone to see another text from Bonnie: *Oh my gosh! Call me!*

She was such a drama queen. I wondered why she didn't ever call me instead of texting me, telling me to call her.

Thirty-nine-year-old Bonnie Fattori was a voluptuous Italian princess and Greek goddess all wrapped up in one person. She had beautiful long, dark-brown hair with gorgeous golden highlights. Even after having two children, she still had that perfect hourglass figure that women like me only dream about. Her deep brown eyes and plump lips made men fall out of their chairs when she walked by.

I was probably Bonnie's opposite in looks. I stood ten inches shorter than Bonnie when she wore her four-inch stiletto heels and I had blonde hair and green eyes. I was still thin, even though I put on a few pounds too many when I was pregnant. Not that I was bad looking, but I was more cute and perky compared to Bonnie, who was sexy and sultry.

I dialed her number.

"What now? Just kidding," I said with a giggle.

"Oh my god, Chelsey, the FBI was here. They came in with warrants and confiscated various records and computers. They served me with some papers, asking for a whole bunch of stuff, like text messages and cell phone records. How on Earth am I supposed to get that?"

Oh my word, she wasn't such a drama queen after all, was she? I was speechless.

"Uh, did you give it to the town attorney?"

"Yes, but you know how he is—he *never* responds to me."

Our town attorney was Colby Betts III. He was a nice guy, but he was from the Deep South and people from his neck of the woods were much more laid back than us Jersey folks. Colby was a Sunday driver on an autobahn. It wasn't that he *never* responded; it just took him forever to respond. In his mind, nothing was urgent. In our minds, everything was urgent. His looks reminded me of Colonel Sanders, but he had longer hair. His great, great grandfather was a Confederate soldier. He commonly wore a white or light-colored suit and vest. He also loved to wear a white Stetson, which he bought when he vacationed in Texas last year.

"Do you know why they were there or who they were after?" I asked her.

"I don't know! They took a bunch of files and took lots of pictures of documents, like the marriage license book, receipt books, and the mayor's files. They didn't really say what they wanted."

"Geez, Bonnie! I'm glad I'm not there! But seriously, I once heard of a town that was investigated because some guy was married to three different women. Maybe they were looking to see if the mayor married someone who turned out to be a polygamist. Call the cell phone company, I guess, and ask them how to go about getting records from them. Call me back and let me know what happens."

Before hanging up with Bonnie, I relayed the news about Randy to her. I asked her if she would tell everyone at work so that I didn't have to be the one to explain it repeatedly. I told her to make sure no one asked me about him when I returned to work. It was too painful for me to think of my baby girl growing up without a father and I didn't want to discuss it with anyone.

On Tuesday, April 3rd, the headlines in the local rag paper, the *Lagoon Tribune*, screamed *"FBI Raids Town Hall!"* I kept reading. *"Sunshine Twp. - FBI agents stormed into Town Hall yesterday and left with several boxes in hand. Sources close to the investigation say that they were working on a tip about government corruption, however, they would not elaborate. No arrests were made. Mayor Frita O'Donnell could not be reached for comment."*

Mayor Frita O'Donnell was in her fifties, short in stature, and plump in physique. Time hadn't been as kind to her as it had been to other people her age. She didn't own any cosmetics. Once she cut her long locks and dyed her buzz cut black, she was more masculine looking than usual. She had been mayor for the past nineteen years. Well, except for that one year, 2003 to be exact, when she didn't get elected, and Pizza Joe, i.e. Joe Marino, owner of Pizza Joe's restaurant, took over. After a year, Pizza Joe decided being mayor wasn't a good fit for him and Mayor O'Donnell was appointed to fill his unexpired term.

A day later, I noticed that Mayor O'Donnell had issued a press release. That was thanks to the fact that I had subscribed to the town's e-mail list and "liked" their Facebook page in an effort to keep up with what was going on in Sunshine when I was on leave. It said something about the FBI investigation being a routine matter, there was no wrongdoing on the part of the town or any of its officials, and that the mayor and staff of Sunshine were fully cooperating with the FBI.

I closed the email on my Android. I couldn't help but feel glad that I didn't have to deal with the FBI. I was happy to be off from work. I was fairly depressed for the first month after the baby was born, due to that deadbeat of an ex-fiancé who dropped us both when we needed him the most. At least the newspaper, e-mails, and Facebook were keeping my mind off my personal life. I was too busy and sleep deprived most days anyway to dwell on the fact that some loser I used to love wasn't man enough to stick around. Because we had been arguing for eight out of the nine months that I was pregnant, I kind of knew the end of us was in sight. I cried for ninety percent of my pregnancy and I was all cried out. I had moved on to my angry phase. Plus, I had always been sort of a strong, independent woman and I knew that Mandy and I would be better off in the long run.

I never heard back from Bonnie. I guess she figured it all out on her own or maybe she went shopping to ease her stress. Bonnie was a big shopper. Her shopping habits were so out of control that her husband made her get a job to support her addiction to clothes and accessories. She lived in one of those beachfront mini-mansions. She was married to a neurosurgeon. I was sometimes jealous of her lifestyle, but I couldn't hold it against her because she was such a caring person.

It was hard not to feel bad for Bonnie right now with this new craziness at work that she had to deal with. I missed a lot of our yearly crunch times in the office like issuing dog licenses, which were due in January, budget time, beach badges in the spring, and the June Primary Election. Bonnie was stuck handling it all. I hoped that Bonnie was getting extra help from other departments so she could cope with it all. I wished for the insanity at work to fade over the next few months before I was finished with my leave of absence.

# 2

June 20th was the first official day of summer and also my first day back at work. Thanks to the laws in New Jersey, I was able to take an extended leave for disability in order to care for a new baby. The morning was hectic. This was my first time trying to wake up to feed and change the baby, in addition to getting myself together while she screamed her head off. I loaded Mandy into the car along with a hundred baby items and headed to my parents' house. My parents had agreed to provide day care for Mandy, which was convenient for me because they only lived a few minutes away from my office.

The job as municipal clerk could best be described as a jack-of-all-trades. It was especially true in a smaller town, where we didn't have enough employees to handle all the positions that are required in local government. According to the New Jersey Legislature, the municipal clerk was the chief custodian of records, the chief elections official, the secretary to the governing body and the chief registrar of voters. Without having our own health, human resources, and purchasing departments, I was also in charge of vital statistics, personnel issues, budget basics, and so many other things, it would take me years to explain it all. Three years, to be exact. That's how long it took me to get through the classes at Rutgers University to obtain the prestigious Registered Municipal Clerk certification. The state exam was the worst test I ever took in my life, inclusive of all my college finals. I personally think it is equivalent to the bar exam. It's not the easiest job in the world, but I love it. I am a hard worker and I like that the office is so hectic all the time. It makes the day go by quickly.

I saw the job posting for the position of municipal clerk for the Town of Sunshine a little over a year ago. This rare opportunity was available because their town clerk of thirty years retired. I thought it would be perfect for me since I knew the town like the back of my hand, had a college degree, and five years of experience as a Deputy Clerk. I thought it was the start of a new chapter in my life. I was excited to be working closer to home, taking the next step in my career and starting a family. That is, until Randy tainted my outlook.

I felt really bad when I found out I was pregnant, having only accepted the job four months prior. I was scared to tell them about my news since I was still only on probation. I knew they couldn't fire me, but I didn't want to make them angry. Once I was twelve weeks along, I spilled my secret and, to my surprise, everyone was supportive. My thoughts about them being angry were completely unrealistic and unwarranted. That's one of the reasons I liked working there so much, I had the nicest coworkers; they were like my extended family. Being a single mom, it meant the world to me to have a good support network like the one I had at Sunshine.

Mom and Dad were waiting on the porch. They were so excited to be spending the day with their only grandchild. Dad was in his wife-beater tank top and long khaki shorts. His beer belly protruded from his thin frame. He was mostly bald now, but still had some blonde hair left on the sides. Mom was in a blue and white striped short-sleeved shirt and white capri pants. She still looked young for a woman in her fifties. She kept her hair dyed golden blonde and cut into a bob that was longer in the front. She loved to walk, which contributed to her slender body and lean legs.

"Now, don't you worry," Mom said in her caring voice. "Mandy will be fine today." My dad also told me not to worry and wished me good luck at work. "I'm making my famous fish sauce for dinner tonight," Dad said. He did make great fish sauce—loaded with clams, scallops, and shrimp on top of angel hair pasta. Yum.

I unloaded the mounds of Mandy's necessities into my parents' living room. I kissed my daughter's sweet little chubby cheeks and said, "Mommy loves Mandy" before I left. I wanted to cry when I turned to leave the house. This was my first full day leaving her. I was sad, but not worried. I knew my parents would take good care of her. I was just missing her already.

I pulled up into the parking lot at the municipal building, got out of my car, straightened up my black pencil skirt and white blouse, and then headed into the main doors.

The Municipal Complex was a block away from the ocean on Beach Boulevard and contained the municipal building, the police station, the senior center, and the lifeguard headquarters. The firehouse was a half mile away on Main Street. There are only a handful of full-time employees like me. The rest of our employees were all part-time, temp workers, or contractors, including the mayor and council members.

When I first became pregnant, I would bring a picnic with me to work so I could sit on my blanket, watching the waves in the ocean while I enjoyed my hour-long lunch. By July, the heat (and everything else) would make me nauseous. That was part of the reason why I spilled the beans about my bun in the oven. People were starting to wonder why I was constantly running to the ladies' room with my hand cupped over my mouth.

I went through the lobby and into the clerk's office. The office was the same as I had left it six months ago. The clerk's office sat to the left of the main doors. For safety, we had a large open window with a counter facing the lobby of the building, which allowed us to wait on the public without them being inside our space. In reality, it wasn't all that safe; someone could jump right through the window. I suppose it provided a barrier so that people couldn't easily reach in, grab the money, and run. The staff entrance for the office was off to the right side of the window. My personal office was situated in the rear of the inside of the clerk's office, to the right of the staff entrance.

*"Authorized Personnel Only – Do Not Enter"* was written on a green sign attached to the staff entrance. Bonnie always joked that the sign was reversed and that it was really telling us authorized personnel not to enter and therefore, we shouldn't have to come to work today.

When I made my grand entrance, Bonnie hugged me and said, "I'm happy you're back. Now you get to deal with Mr. Trigger's five-hour weekly visits." She laughed, then asked me to join her in the kitchen for a cup of coffee. When we walked in, I was greeted by the rest of my coworkers, who threw me a little welcome back party. Even the mayor was there, which was surprising to me because she didn't normally attend our staff events. Everyone congratulated me and bought baby presents. Bonnie whispered in my ear, "Don't eat the brownies."

"Why not?" I asked her.

"Rodney made them."

Enough said. I wouldn't be eating the brownies. Rodney Wilson was our town administrator. He was fifty-eight years old and had medical issues that no one would talk about because it upset him so much. Rodney missed a lot of work due to his illness. I knew he had a prescription for medical marijuana. I wasn't sure if he was supposed to be indulging in it during work hours, but I suspected he sometimes ate the brownies, so to speak. On his bad days, his hands would shake and he was grumpy. On a good day, his eyes were red; he was calm, cheery, and had the munchies. He was a nice fellow nonetheless and I appreciated his baking effort for me, but I wasn't taking any chances.

Bonnie had previously told me the story of the first time Rodney brought in brownies. Everyone ate them, not knowing any better. Needless to say, work was not getting done! It appeared a resident was not pleased with the giggling brood of municipal employees and called the mayor to complain. The mayor was tied up at her full-time job, so she sent the town attorney to find out what was going on in Town Hall that day.

The tax collector was busy satisfying her munchies. The chief financial officer was in a state of paranoia. Rodney was continually placing drops in his red eyes. Bonnie was talking non-stop. They were all in the clerk's office together. When Mr. Betts arrived and found them, he said, "What on God's good Earth is going on around here? It's like all y'all did today was take your happy pills."

With his southern drawl, bolero tie, and cowboy hat, they couldn't control their giggles.

"C'mon now, y'all, stop this circus and get back to work," Betts told them.

They all looked at each other and burst into laughter.

"Gosh dang it, will someone please tell me what is going on?" Betts pleaded. "Y'all are making me madder than an oinker at the pig wrestlin' contest."

I believe Rodney fell right off his chair after that comment. Bonnie peed herself a little.

Now, Betts is a smart man, so he eventually figured out exactly what had happened. They were all put on probation for three months. They didn't get fired because it wasn't one hundred percent their faults for being high on the job. They were told if there was ever another "accident" like this one, they'd all be collecting unemployment. Since then, they couldn't be sure whether or not Rodney was adding his secret ingredient to his baking, so no one would take the risk and indulge in his goodies. I never did understand why Rodney got off the hook. I often wondered if the story was even true or if Bonnie was just yanking my chain.

After an hour of opening presents and talking about the baby, I decided it was time to get back into the swing of work. There was a council meeting next week and the agenda deadline was in two days. It was always crazy on agenda weeks. I draft the majority of the items that the council members will be voting on, including resolutions and ordinances, then I coordinate all the paperwork for Bonnie to scan.

The council went green and approved the purchase of iPads in the budget this year, which made our lives a little easier. Instead of having to use reams of paper to copy agenda items, we could now email materials to those who needed them.

As I turned to leave the party, I heard Rodney say, "Chelsey, aren't you going to have one of my brownies? I'm a good baker, you know."

"Oh sure, Rod. I'm stuffed right now from the bagels and muffins, but I'll take one back to my desk for later," I told him. Then I poured myself a glass of orange juice, wrapped a brownie in a napkin, and brought them with me. When the coast was clear, I pitched the brownie into the wastebasket.

I was in the middle of pulling a file out for an agenda item when the fire alarm went off. Bonnie had stepped out of the office so I grabbed both of our purses and hustled out of the building. I realized that no one else seemed to be moving. Quite a few minutes later, other employees strolled leisurely out of the door. I walked over to Bonnie and handed her purse to her.

"I hope this isn't a real fire; everyone would have died from smoke inhalation," I said to her.

"Ever since we had the fire in the courtroom, these darn alarms go off at least once a week. The alarms didn't work when we needed them and now they work when we don't need them."

The fire engine pulled into our lot and several calendar-worthy firemen jumped off and entered the municipal building.

"The advantage to the false alarms is the eye candy," Bonnie said.

"You're married," I responded.

"I may be married, but I'm not dead. I can look. They give me something to fantasize about when I'm in bed with my husband."

"Geez, Bonnie! Too much information."

"Just you wait until you've been married as long as I have. You need to come up with fresh ideas to keep the romance alive."

"No chance of me getting married any time soon."

"Don't talk like that. You'll meet someone."

"I don't need someone right now."

The firemen gave the all-clear for us to go back to work. When I got into my office, I glanced up and saw someone approaching the counter.

"Did I miss the party?"

Officer Michael Williams was six feet, six inches tall and had movie-star good looks. He was probably a couple of years younger than I was. He had dark hair, a tan complexion, and what I imagined to be the perfectly chiseled body with rock hard abs under that uniform. The uniform made him seem all the sexier to me. His eyes were a deep rich blue and mesmerizing. He was fairly new to the police force, having started working there only a couple of months after I had started. He seemed like he came from a nice family. I had met his parents on his first day of work, when he was sworn in. It's my job to administer the Oaths of Office to the new hires. I sometimes like my job very much!

"No, Mike, there's still some food in the kitchen. Help yourself," I told him.

"Welcome back, Chelsey."

I melted. He was so handsome. I watched him as he turned toward the break room. I saw Mayor O'Donnell grab his arm and start talking to him on the way in. I guess it's smart to be chummy with the mayor. Job security.

"I saw that!" Bonnie said with a smirk.

"Saw what?"

"The way you looked at him."

"How did I look at him?"

"Like you want him for lunch."

"You shouldn't talk; I needed to find a tissue to wipe the drool oozing down your face when those firemen jumped out of the truck."

"And I admitted to that. I'm not ashamed. You should go to the kitchen and try to talk to him."

"Oh, geez, Bonnie. I recently had a baby. I was engaged to another man just five months ago. The last thing I need right now is another man in my life. Besides, I'm in bed by eight every night. How would I have time to go on a date?"

"I'd be thrilled to babysit for you. Did you get a load of how big his hands are?" Bonnie asked.

"No, I didn't look at his hands. What does that have to do with anything?"

"You know…the bigger the hands, the bigger the…"

I cut her off there. I put my fingers in my ears and said, "La la la la, I can't hear you."

She laughed. "Stop the act, Ms. Not-So-Prim and Proper. I'm on to you. You can't tell me you wouldn't rip off his clothes and have your way with him if you could."

"Bonnie, I think this is a form of sexual harassment in the work place," I joked. "Now, get back to work."

I looked out of the window and saw Mayor O'Donnell leaving from the kitchen. "Welcome back, Chelsey. We all missed you very much while you were gone."

"Thanks, Mayor," I called out. She was so sweet. It was good to be back. I headed back into my office to get caught up with the five hundred plus emails that were sitting in my inbox.

When four thirty came, I felt so tired. I was definitely not back in the swing of things just yet. Regardless of my exhaustion, I was excited to go get my little baby girl. I was also looking forward to Dad's fish sauce. I locked up the office and said good-bye to Bonnie. Bonnie asked how I felt after my first day back. "Like I could sleep for a week," I said.

"Well, at least Mr. Triggers didn't bother you on your fist day."

"Is he really that bad?" I asked

"Worse!" she replied.

# 3

My first council meeting back to the job was also my first taste of Mr. Triggers. I figured out who he was from the description Bonnie gave me. I think it was his eyes that gave it away. He *did* have crazy eyes. He was one of the first residents to show up that evening.

It was the first time I was back in the courtroom since it had caught fire. It was set up much nicer than before. It was a square room with fifty brand new blue chairs facing a dais. The dais was one step up from the seating area and it was completely redone in oak. There was seating for the mayor, eight council members, and me on the dais. The mayor's seat was in the middle. My seat was next to the emergency exit.

Overly wide double doors were installed at the back of the room and led outside. There was a side door, which allowed entrance to the main lobby of the municipal building. The doors were always left open during a meeting.

New ocean-colored carpet had been installed and the walls were painted a fresh coat of beige. I think the color blue was picked to have a calming effect, but I don't think the color psychologists told anyone that the initial feelings of calm quickly dissipate once a council meeting begins.

Metal detectors surrounded the main courtroom entrance. There was a guard scanning residents as they came into the meeting. The metal detectors were added after an incident in another state was publicized. A Senator was shot and killed during a public meeting. The town decided to take precautions to prevent such a tragic incident in Sunshine.

When the mayor called for public participation, Triggers was the first up to the microphone. After forty-five minutes of rambling about the dunes and the red tape involved with government, Mayor O'Donnell interrupted him, "You've been here frequently, taking up hours of everyone's time. What is your point?"

I suddenly perked up. The mayor didn't normally cut off members of the public who spoke at council meetings. She usually let them drone on and on.

Triggers turned three shades of red. "I have a right to speak and you have no right to interrupt me. Now, as I was saying…"

The mayor interrupted again. "Mr. Triggers, we have heard this over and over and we have told you that we are not going to install dunes on someone's private property. This is a council meeting and while it is okay to make a comment, it is not okay to give a dissertation. Now, unless you are going to say something new, this topic is finished."

Triggers clenched his teeth together. "I am trying to explain the danger that can occur to our homes because there are no dunes protecting my street and you keep throwing your stupid red tape at me to get me to go away.

I'm sure if I were a councilman, or one of your political buddies, I'd have those dunes by now. If you don't install the dunes and we have a flood, our homes will be ruined and you don't..."

Mayor O'Donnell struck the gavel several times. "Mr. Triggers, we do not use favoritism and I'm insulted at your insinuation. We *have* tried to help you. I personally met with the homeowner, Mr. Bill Bradford, and he does not wish for dunes to be placed on his property. We have had appraisals done on the property and it is too cost prohibitive for the town to condemn the land in order to install the dunes. We have spoken to engineers about a way to place the dunes on public land so as to not block Mr. Bradford's view. We have investigated the legal aspects of everything. You know this, you have been told this, and you have also been informed that it is our decision that we are not installing dunes at this time. We thank you for your comments, but we are now moving on with the meeting."

Triggers rolled up his papers and pointed them at Mayor O'Donnell. "I am not finished, I will be back, and you will not get rid of me so easily. You have been warned!" Then he stormed out of the room.

The rest of the council meeting was unexciting in comparison. When the meeting was over, I joked to the mayor, "I'm happy I sit near the emergency exit. When Mr. Triggers comes back with a gun and points it at you, I can duck and make a quick getaway."

Mayor O'Donnell chuckled. "I know, Chelsey, someone has to be the heavy hand. Might as well be me." I was silently relieved that we had metal detectors and a guard at the meetings. When I joked with the mayor, I was only half joking. Triggers seemed scary to me.

I was home by ten thirty that night. Mandy was sound asleep in her crib and my dad was sound asleep in front of the TV. I tiptoed past him in an effort not to wake him, but he heard me anyway.

"Hi. How was the meeting?" he said in a sleepy voice.

"You mean besides the nut job who wants his dunes installed?"

"Oh, he was there?" he asked. "What did he say?"

"I don't know, he went on and on for forty-five minutes. I tuned it out. The mayor interrupted him in the middle of it. He was mad about that. Nothing else really happened. Was Mandy good?"

"Yeah, she was good. She fell asleep around seven."

"Oh good, I'm heading to bed. Are you going to sleep on the couch or go home? I'm exhausted from working all week. I'm not used to it from being home on maternity leave."

"I'm going to head home. My back can't take sleeping on the couch these days. I am getting old, you know. I'll let myself out and lock up for you."

I hardly considered my father old at fifty-nine years of age. He retired seven years ago by taking a buyout from his job at the Turnpike Authority, which left him bored and feeling older than he was.

"Thanks for babysitting. I love you, Dad," I said as I went to my room and drifted off to sleep.

Morning came much too early for me. Mandy woke me up at five a.m. daily. She was more reliable than an alarm clock. I rolled out of bed, threw my shoulder-length hair into a ponytail holder, and went to Mandy's room. I changed her diaper, got her dressed, and made her a bottle. I loved her curly blonde hair. My hair was poker straight, so I was not sure where she got her curls from. It was even curlier in the humidity that we were having. I enjoyed this little quiet time with her, when she was cuddled in my arms, taking her morning feeding. She liked to play with my hair and she'd push my head to one side to grab hold of my ponytail. Evenings after work were incredibly hectic. I'd pick her up, get home, feed her, make dinner, eat, give her a bath, change her, and get her to bed. It always felt like a whirlwind. I missed the laid-back days when I wasn't working. A part-time job would give me my much-needed adult interaction time and a good amount of time to spend with my daughter. Working full-time or not working at all seemed to me to be too much one way or another and I would have much preferred a happy medium. Oh well, I could stop dreaming, because part-time work was out of the question for me financially and due to the fact that I needed health benefits.

After I got ready for work, I loaded Mandy into the car and off we went to my parents' house. The causeway was unusually backed up this morning. "Oh, that's right, I had forgotten it was the closest weekend to Fourth of July and there would be a lot of travelers this morning," I told Mandy, even though she couldn't understand me. I raced down Main Street, turned onto Thirteenth, and pulled into their driveway. My father was standing at the porch door. "You're late," he said.

"I know, I know. Her food is all in the bag, I have to run," I said as I handed Mandy to him, then hurried back to the driveway. "Mommy loves Mandy, bye, bye." I waved as I got back in the car and sped over to work. I grabbed my keys and my purse and hustled into the building, to be greeted by Mr. Triggers waiting anxiously at the clerk's office window. He was holding a large rock that was bigger than a tennis ball, but smaller than a basketball.

*Oh, what a great way to start the day,* I thought. *And what is with the rock? A pet rock, perhaps?* I had forgotten that Bonnie had a scheduled vacation day (aka shopping day) for today. It was the morning after the meeting, I was running late, I had a ton of work to get done, and now I had to deal with *him.* On top of that, he smelled like he spent the night in a trashcan.

"Good morning," I said, trying to hold my breath so his odor didn't penetrate my nostrils. I wrestled with my keys to get the office door opened as quickly as possible.

Mr. Triggers frowned. "You're late," he proclaimed.

"Traffic," I said. "How can I help you?"

"Are you as stupid as the other girl who works here?"

I was taken aback by his rudeness and I found myself at a loss for words.

"I want to see copies of all resolutions adopted regarding the beach from nineteen sixty to present."

"All of them?" I asked.

"Yes, all of them! There should only be a few pages."

I asked him to fill out a Request for Records form and I explained that there were thousands of them; not a few pages. I told him that I would have to order most of them from archives.

"Ah, what do you know? More red tape—I have to fill out a form. How long will they take to get here? I want to see them now."

"Oh, I'm terribly sorry. It won't be today."

I explained that they were in storage at an off-site facility. He glared at me. "This is a classic example of government red tape and how stupid you government employees are! I want them now, I have a right to see them, and I will wait here at this window until they get here."

Okay, now what? I couldn't possibly get the company we used for storage to deliver them today.

"Perhaps if you tell me what you are looking for, I might be able to locate the particular resolution you need; all resolutions about the beach is a broad topic."

"Your feeble little mind wouldn't be able to understand what I'm looking for," Mr. Triggers announced.

"Well, I can't get them today. Would you be able to come back on Monday?" I asked. His insults were starting to bother me.

"I don't want them on Monday. I have free time today, and I want them today. This is just more of your red tape and I'm not going to fall for it."

I did a mental eye roll and tried again. "The company we use does not have same-day service. I will send the request for the boxes over now and I will have them on the next business day, which is Monday. Can you come here on Monday or another day next week?"

Triggers continued to be argumentative. I told him I would get him the most recent documents I had referencing the beach and I started to walk away. He yelled at me and slammed down his rock with a loud bang. He pointed, saying, "I'm not done speaking yet!"

The slamming of the rock alarmed me. I wondered if he would pick it up and throw it at me. I entertained the idea of calling the police. I stopped in my tracks and waited for him to speak. He didn't say anything. I waited two more minutes, which seemed more like a half hour. Then I said, "I will be right back."

I returned with seven file folders containing various resolutions and reports about the beach and beach erosion and handed them to him over the counter, telling him to call me if he needed something copied. I left the window and proceeded to my personal office.

I put my purse in my desk drawer, took a deep breath, and counted to ten. I had to calm myself down, I was so aggravated. After fifteen minutes, I peeked out of my office to find Mr. Triggers intently perusing the files. His dark eyes gave me the chills. I didn't like this man and I didn't trust him. I decided to quietly call the police non-emergency number.

"Dispatcher Twenty-four."

"This is Chelsey Alton, the Town Clerk," I whispered. "I don't want to be an alarmist, but Mr. Triggers is at my window, holding a large rock, going through records. I'm here in my office alone today. I don't think he will pull any stunts, but I'm feeling a little nervous. Do you think you could send someone over to periodically check on me?"

"Ten-four, copy that," the dispatcher said before he hung up.

I waited for another ten minutes, then peered out toward the window again. He was still there. I felt like I couldn't get any work done because I had to keep my eye on him. I decided to bring my supplies and papers out to Bonnie's desk so I could keep watch.

I saw a police officer walk by the window and look over Triggers' shoulder. I waved. He gave me a thumbs up with the look of a question mark on his face. I gave him a nod to let him know I was okay.

Thirty more minutes passed. Triggers finally looked calm. Perhaps, since he saw the volume of records I handed him, he finally believed that I couldn't store all those documents from nineteen sixty in this small office. I chuckled at the thought of how clueless he was—he actually thought there were only going to be few pages. Another person who didn't have any idea about how much work we do around here.

He remained at the counter for about five hours straight. A different police officer took a walk through the building every thirty minutes or so. This made me feel more at ease. I'm not exactly sure when Triggers finally left, sometime around two fifteen in the afternoon. After all that time, he didn't take copies of anything, but I saw him periodically making notes for himself. I didn't know if he was coming back for the day or what was going on. I ordered the other files from storage and went about my day.

When four thirty rolled around, I realized that Triggers had not returned and I was thankful for that. My stomach was growling. I hadn't been able to leave the office for lunch since that nut was at my office window for such a long time. My dad was making pot roast tonight. The thought of a yummy meal and a nice weekend waiting was enough to make me bounce out of the door as fast as I could.

As I headed out to my car, I could see Officer Williams across the parking lot. He waved. My knees went weak. I waved back. *Oh, he's so dreamy.* "Stop it Chelsey, stop it," I said to myself, "I do not like him, I do not like him."

My train of thought was cut short by the mayor's voice. "Hi, Chelsey! How's the baby?" She was always so thoughtful.

"She's great; thanks for asking. Do you need my help with anything?"

"No, I'm fine. I have a meeting to get to at the police station."

"Oh, I wanted to ask you, how did everything turn out with the FBI? I missed a lot; I was out for so long."

"Case of mistaken identity. Nothing to be concerned with."

"Okay, well, I hope your meeting doesn't last too long. Take care!" I said and I waved as I drove off to my parents' house.

# 4

My alarm clock went off at five-o-three a.m. Perhaps alarm clock wasn't a nice nickname, but that was my little Mandy—an early riser. I shuffled into her bedroom and lifted her out of the crib. I changed her and dressed her in her turquoise elephant shirt and skirt. I put a little turquoise clip bow in her blonde curls, then took her picture with my cell phone. She looked so cute, I had to upload it to Facebook.

I carried her into the kitchen and fed her breakfast. The doctor let me start feeding her cereal recently and she loved it. I left her in her swing to take a nap while I got showered and dressed for work. I reminded myself to leave early today, since it was only two days before the Fourth of July and there would be a lot of visitors on the island this week. I dressed in a beige A-line skirt and black short-sleeved top with my black slingbacks.

Traffic was heavy, as I predicted, but I still made it to work on time. I turned off the ignition and threw my purse over my shoulder. The sun was shining and it wasn't too humid for a July morning. I predicted it would be a good day today. I walked into the lobby and saw Bonnie standing in the doorway to our office with Detective Jose Texidoro.

Detective Texidoro, or as I called him, "Tex," was a veteran on our police force. He had started as a dispatcher when he was twenty years old. He was now forty-six and he could retire with a nice pension and full medical benefits whenever he wanted. He was five feet, eight inches tall, Spanish, and had a little beer belly. Tex had a sarcastic personality, in a "trying to be funny" sense. We joked around a lot and he often had me in stitches.

Tex and his wife Stephanie had been close friends of my family for as long as I could remember. His parents and my parents were neighbors back in the day before I was born. My mother sort of "adopted" him in his twenties when his parents passed away in a tragic car accident, supplying him with plenty of food and a substitute family.

He and Bonnie looked very serious. As I approached them, Bonnie turned to me and said, "Don't freak out." Confused, I asked, "What's going on?" As I looked past them in the office, I saw papers and books in complete disarray covering the floor. Drawers were left open with files sticking out of them. The cash box was on the floor and empty. A chair was tipped over and Bonnie's computer was busted to smithereens.

My face dropped. I looked at Tex. He turned to me and said, chuckling, "Let me guess, you and Bonnie were fighting over the last of Rodney's brownies."

"Not funny."

"Okay, then, seriously, you two have to stay out of the office for now. This is a crime scene. We'll dust for fingerprints and see if there is any trace of evidence that was left behind. We noticed the money is gone. When we are done, I will need you to try to figure out if anything else is missing. Meanwhile, I want to get a statement from you."

A couple of officers were already in the office bagging items and hanging up yellow crime scene tape across the doorway. Tex asked me what time I left on Friday.

"Four thirty, and I saw the mayor in the parking lot on her way to a meeting. She could vouch for me," I said.

"Easy there, Tonto. I wasn't accusing you of anything. You could take the money without ransacking the office. Now, did you see anyone in or around the building on that was unusual?" Tex asked.

"Unusual? Do you mean like Robert Triggers sitting at my window for five straight hours with his pet rock, then disappearing without saying a word?"

"Yes, kind of like that."

"I wasn't here over the weekend and the only unusual person that was in on Friday was Mr. Triggers, but police officers kept walking by to make sure I was safe. You could ask them if anyone saw him leave, because I didn't see where he went."

"What time do you think he left?"

"He left my window about two o'clock or a little after."

Tex interrogated me some more about Mr. Triggers. The interrogation included questions about his demeanor. I told Tex that Triggers seemed upset at first that I couldn't give him all the records he had wanted on Friday. Maybe he broke in looking for them. Perhaps he thought I was lying about getting the records from off-site storage.

I wondered if Triggers did this. He certainly knew what our office hours were. I tried to envision how he got in the building. I started making up scenarios in my head of the crime. I imagined him breaking through a window after dark dressed all in black, wearing a ski mask. I pictured Triggers smashing the door handle with his rock. Maybe he stumbled on the money by accident while looking for records when he broke the lock on the file cabinet where we keep the cash box. So much for my prediction that today was going to be a good day.

I was snapped back into reality with the sound of Bonnie's voice. "Earth to Chelsey."

"Huh?"

"Where did you go just now?" she asked.

"I don't know. I'm thinking about whether or not Triggers broke in here."

"Maybe you should invest in a more secure safe for the cash or anything of value," Tex suggested.

"Maybe things happened for a reason—maybe this break-in is enough to convince the powers that be to put money in the budget for a safe," I said.

"If there anything else you think of, just call me."

"Wait, before you leave…how did they break in?"

"Your door was kicked or pushed in. It's so lightweight, it wouldn't take much strength to bust open. The main building doors were either left open or someone knew how to open door locks without a key."

"Okay, thanks." So much for my daydream about how the crime occurred. I probably wouldn't have made a great detective. I started to think about how I was going to get my work done for the day without having access to the office or my desk. Rodney was out on

leave for a couple of weeks again, so I was the one temporarily in charge and as much as I wanted to, I couldn't call it a day and head home. I supposed I could work at Rodney's desk, since he was out.

I went into the Rodney's office for the remainder of the day. First on my agenda was to call the mayor. I dialed her from my cell phone to bring her up to speed on what happened. I told her to expect a phone call from Tex. She was disturbed by the news, but relieved that no one was around to get hurt during the break-in. I explained to her that the locks on the main doors might have been picked and that the door to the clerk's office appeared to be kicked in because it was so flimsy. She agreed with me about my suspicion that Mr. Triggers was behind the robbery.

Mayor O'Donnell told me to look into the cost getting an alarm system, better locks, and a stronger door that was less likely to be kicked in. I asked her if I could also look into getting a safe and she agreed. I knew this was all pointless. I would go through the trouble of spending time getting quotes, drafting the proper paperwork, and reviewing where there were funds available for these purchases with our CFO. Then, I would present everything at a council meeting. Council would say there is no money in this year's budget and they would vote *no* on the purchases. I often felt the current group of elected officials was penny-wise and pound-foolish. If there were better security to begin with, then there would be less money spent in OT for the police and no money spent on the damages to the building.

While I was on the phone with the mayor, the storage company showed up with the boxes I had ordered for Mr. Triggers. Bonnie informed me about their arrival and I followed her into the lobby.

"I didn't know where to put them all," Bonnie said.

The boxes were scattered all over the lobby. I went back to Rodney's desk and sent a work-order via email requesting a table and some help with moving boxes around from public works.

Within forty minutes, several public works employees found me in Rodney's office and offered to help move the boxes. I walked them down the hallway and pushed open the door to the lobby. I turned around to show them where I wanted the table set up, took a step back, and next thing I knew, I tripped over one of the boxes and fell flat on my back. It wouldn't have been so bad, except that I was fairly sure that all three men from public works got a sneak peek at my white cotton panties. I turned eight shades of red and tried to scramble to my feet. Bonnie was almost on the floor herself, laughing at me. I cursed Mr. Triggers in my head for making me bring the darn boxes over.

"You can claim workman's comp," one of the guys said, "We were all witnesses!"

"I'm fine," I managed to muster.

I showed them where I wanted the boxes moved and where the table should go. I figured Mr. Triggers could sit at the table near the outside of our office so that I could spit on him…er, um, I mean so we could keep an eye on him while he looked through the boxes. I didn't trust him and I wouldn't put it past him to take something.

I hustled back to Rodney's office and closed the door. I needed to hide for a while and nurse my bruised ego back to health.

By the next morning, the police were finished processing the crime scene and we were allowed back in to our office. Bonnie and I started cleaning up and taking inventory. We tried to remember how much money was in the cash box. There was two hundred dollars in there for starters to make change with. Bonnie wasn't in the office on Friday, so she wouldn't have taken in any payments. The receipt books were missing, but I recalled taking twenty-eight dollars for a marriage license and ten dollars for a death certificate. I turned to Bonnie. "This reminds me, before I left for maternity leave, I thought I had ordered more safety paper for the vital records. Did that ever come in?"

"I thought it did. Did you check the birth certificate drawer?"

"I did, but I only saw one package. Did you use up the whole other package?"

Bonnie said she couldn't remember, but she would look into the sequential numbers on the paper when she had time.

I didn't know how we would figure out if any other records were missing. Since I was considered the custodian of records, there are thousands of files in my office. If I discovered that documents were missing, I could recreate the ones that were saved on the network, but for the rest, I wouldn't know where to start.

Later that day, I gave an update to Tex. It indicated that we were missing two hundred thirty-eight dollars in cash, our receipt books, and possibly a package of safety paper. In addition, the computer was destroyed, there was damage to the door and one file cabinet, and I couldn't tell if other records were taken.

"Safety paper?" he asked with a goofy grin on his face. "What the heck is that? Is that the paper that keeps you safe from intruders? If so, it didn't work."

Sarcastically, I responded, "Ha. Ha. Don't quit your day job to become a comedian just yet."

I explained that safety paper is the paper we use to issue vital records—birth, marriage, death, civil union, or domestic partnership certificates. He seemed interested when I explained what they were. I told him that I wasn't actually sure that the safety paper was missing and if it was, I wasn't one hundred percent positive that it wasn't missing before this break-in.

"Are you sure of anything?" he asked.

"I'm sure you can lay off the donuts a tad. I should start calling you 'Chubby' instead of 'Tex.'"

"Oh, bring it on, sister. You sure you wanna go there? You really want me to tell you that you need to take off that extra baby weight?"

"Hey! At least I have a reason that I gained weight. What is your reason? That Donut Palace is open twenty-four hours?"

"All right. *Touché*. I'm outta here, if you think of anything else that's missing or any other details, let me know. I'll let you know if we find any fingerprints."

A couple of hours later, the office was cleaned up and we were back in business. Bonnie came in to tell me she had tried to research the numbers on the safety paper. She said that she remembered she had opened a pack of paper in

December. I remembered that too, because I always place an order for more whenever we open a pack. The ream of paper that was currently in the drawer was the new pack that I had ordered. Bonnie hadn't remembered to order more paper while I was out on leave. Since the receipt books were missing, she couldn't tell how many certified copies she had issued while I was out.

"Wait! You really think you issued over five hundred copies while I was gone? That's an awful lot," I told her.

We don't have a hospital and we don't have a funeral home. The only time someone orders a birth certificate is when a baby accidentally pops out in the toilet like on an episode of *I Didn't Know I was Pregnant* and that's not very often. Maybe once a year at most. Most death certificates are obtained by the funeral home in the town where they are located, so we issue very few deaths.

"How many marriage and civil union licenses did you have so far this year?" I asked.

Bonnie took out the log for applications. She told me she issued twenty-seven licenses so far. I really didn't think that twenty-seven couples would have ordered fifteen to twenty certified copies each. It occurred to me that the finance department would have a copy of our daily deposits as well as the bank records and probably a list of internal account activity. I was about to call them up when the fire alarms sounded.

"You weren't exaggerating when you said these alarms go off every week, were you?"

"Nope, I wasn't. Time for me to go gawk at men with big hoses."

I rolled my eyes. We headed outside and had to wait for a thumbs up to return to the building before we could get back to work. When we were permitted back inside, I headed over to finance and asked them how much money was in the vital statistics fees account. They reported there was eight hundred ten dollars in the account. Since the cost is ten dollars per copy, that meant we had only issued eighty-one copies. I started to worry. I walked back to Bonnie's desk.

"Bonnie, there are hundreds of sheets missing."

Bonnie looked at me in shock. "How can that be possible?" she asked.

Then we heard whistling. I turned to see out of the window at our front counter and there he was again….a little slice of heaven on Earth. Oh geez, I had to stop thinking like that; I was like a high school girl when he was around.

"Hello, ladies!" Officer Williams said.

We both waved hello.

"So, I heard you had a break-in. Anything missing?"

Bonnie spoke up and said, "Safety paper," after she realized that I seemed to be tongue-tied.

"Don't worry, we'll catch the guy."

Bonnie said, "How do you know it was a guy?"

Williams said, "I'm a cop, I know things. Besides, I can't picture some little petite woman kicking in a door."

To that Bonnie replied, "Have you seen our mayor?"

"Bonnie!" I exclaimed.

Williams laughed.

"Sorry, but she is kind of manly," Bonnie said.

"Not appropriate, Bonnie," I said, then I went back into my office. I mean, it was funny, but I certainly didn't want anyone to hear her making fun of the mayor. I imagine I could permanently lose a deputy if a certain someone overheard her.

"He's gone," Bonnie shouted into my office.

"What are you talking about?"

"You're future ex-husband is gone now and you can stop hiding in your office."

"What do you mean, my future ex-husband? I don't even like him."

"Bull. You *do* like him. It's written all over your face every time he is around. He makes you nervous. I can tell by the way you went hiding in your office."

"I didn't go hiding in my office," I said, insulted.

"You should go out with him."

"Fine, I'll admit, he's 'eye candy,' as you would say. I enjoy the view, but I'm absolutely not interested in going out with him. Also, I seriously doubt he is interested in dating me."

"I have an idea—flash him your panties like you did with public works yesterday, then he'll be interested."

"Oh my god, Bonnie. I can't believe you just said that! I was so embarrassed. And *you*! You did nothing but laugh at me!"

"I couldn't help laughing; it's a natural reaction. What could I have done, anyway?"

"You could have warned me that there was a box behind me. You could have helped me up. You could have jumped in front of my crotch to limit the view."

She laughed. "Since I am so worthless and of no help to you, how about you let me go home early?"

Since I was still in charge, I granted Bonnie her wish and decided to let all of the employees skip their lunches and start the holiday a little early. Tomorrow would be the Fourth of July. Traffic was horrendous on the island. Plus, I felt stressed over the happenings in the office this week and needed a break myself as well.

# 5

Morning comes entirely too early for me these days. I wished I could have slept in on my day off, but that luxury no longer existed with a baby around. My parents invited me and Mandy over for a cookout later on, but first, I was going to take Mandy to Sunshine's annual Independence Day parade. I chose a pair of comfy shorts and a t-shirt to wear with flip-flops. I put Mandy in her pink and orange Hawaiian-print onesie and headed out at nine. The parade didn't start until eleven, but because parking would be a scarce commodity and traffic would be atrocious, I thought it wise to leave early.

I parked in front of my parents' house and went in to wait for the parade to start.

"Hi, Chelsey! Hi, Mandy, baby!" Mom said. "I went to the farmers' market and got all fresh vegetables for later today—Jersey tomatoes, sweet white corn, and zucchini. We also have burgers, hotdogs, and chicken on the grill. I got you a bottle of that wine you like too, that Dornfelder."

"Thanks, Mom!" I said. "Do you want to go to the parade with us?"

"No thanks, sweetie; we have got too much cooking to do around here."

I fed Mandy her bottle, then put her down for a nap. I helped my mother shuck the corn and cut up the zucchini. "Where's Dad?" I asked her.

"I sent him to the grocery store to see what they had for dessert," my mother said.

My dad was still at the store when Mandy woke up from her nap. I changed her diaper and put her in her stroller. I grabbed a beach chair for myself and walked down to Main Street to join the other spectators. I knew Mandy didn't know what was going on yet, but I always loved the parade and I wanted to share my traditions with her, even if she was too young to understand.

It was a small parade, but people came out in droves to see it. The beating drums wafted through the air before I could see any musicians. It was bright and sunny out with a high of eighty-six degrees predicted for the day. The bay breeze kept the temperature comfortable.

A bright red fire engine led the parade. We watched a showcase of colorful and lively floats stream by, created by various local groups including the Boy and Girl Scouts, the Historical Society, and veterans' group. The Boat Club members dressed in pirate costumes. The school marching band had the crowd swaying to the beat. Clowns were throwing sweets and Frisbees, encouraging youngsters to dive after them.

The air smelled like popcorn and hotdogs from street vendors selling their goodies. I was enjoying the sight of the baton twirlers in their adorable red, white and blue costumes when I spotted the first of the classic cars slowly following down Main Street. It was a nineteen sixty-six Ford Mustang convertible painted canary yellow. The mayor was propped up inside the vehicle above the windshield, waving to the crowd.

As she neared us, I saw something sailing through the air toward her. It was hard to make out, but it was white and looked a lot like a golf ball. Then *splat!* An egg hit her in the ear and splattered all over her face. A second egg had already been launched and as she tried to wipe yolk off her face, *splat!* Another one hit her in the head.

The crowd gasped. The mayor ducked down in the car and covered her head with her arms. The driver couldn't go anywhere as the parade was merely inching along. At least ten more eggs pelted the car, its driver, and Mayor O'Donnell. *Splat, splat, splat.* I could hear her cussing and shrieking. Everyone looked around to see where the eggs were coming from. Then I spotted him—Mr. Triggers, holding an empty carton.

Foot patrols had been strolling along the parade route and they caught up to Mr. Triggers, who was leaving the scene. They wrestled him to the ground after he led them on a short foot chase. Mr. Triggers wasn't very speedy at his age and weight. The police caught him quickly.

"Holy shit," I said after it all went down. "Oops, pardon my French." My daughter couldn't talk yet, but I had forgotten that there were other children in the vicinity, who might repeat my colorful language. Then I laughed my butt off.

After the parade, I walked back to my parents' house to find my father busy putting burgers on the grill. My mother was preparing a tomato salad.

"You're not going to believe what just happened!" I said to my mother. I told her the story, and she laughed too.

I found my cousins, James and Daisy Primer, out on the back patio watching my dad do the grilling. They had driven in from Lawrenceville for the day. Detective Texidoro and his wife, Stephanie, were also joining us for lunch. When they arrived, I told them the tale of a dozen eggs and we all got a good laugh.

I helped myself to a glass of wine, saying "I could use a little wine this week," to no one in particular. I was only back to work for two weeks and I already had the urge to have a drink. I hadn't had a drink in forever. I decided to stop breastfeeding the other day. It was fine while I was home with the baby, but I found it to be too cumbersome to pump now that I was back to work.

"So, how were your first couple of weeks back to work?" Stephanie asked me.

"Do you mean besides a robbery, a lunatic resident, and the fact that I'm acting administrator this week? Fantastic," I said with a hint of sarcasm in my voice. I turned to Tex, "Any leads yet on our intruder?"

Tex told me that there were no leads yet and that the fingerprints were still being processed.

"Did you ask the mayor if she saw anyone strange lurking around?"

"I did and she did not."

We agreed to stop talking shop and enjoy the day. My cousins lived more than an hour away and we didn't see them as often as we liked, so we didn't need to bore them with our work conversation.

"By the way, Chelsey," Stephanie said. "Jose and I have a friend that I am going to set you up with."

*Oh no,* I thought. I could feel my face getting warm. I started fanning myself with an empty paper plate that was on the picnic table in front of me. Were they talking about setting me up with Officer Williams? My heart started beating faster at the thought.

"Well, I don't particularly want to be set up."

"Look, you are single now and we have a great guy for you. He's handsome, successful, and he loves kids. What could it hurt to get out for one night? You admitted you were stressed about work. You need some fun."

My mom piped in, "I'll watch the baby for you, Chelsey." I glared at her as if to tell her not to do me any favors.

"I don't know," I said. "Who are we talking about here?"

"His name is Kristof Beck and he owns Bratz Restaurant," Tex told me.

I was a little disappointed. I guess Bonnie put the idea in my head about going on a date with Officer Williams and as much as I tried to deny it, I was very attracted to him.

"Bratz? Where is that? I never heard of it. And what kind of a name is Kristof?"

"It's German," Tex said. "And the restaurant is a German place with specialty Bratwurst and German beers. It's in Jackson Township near Great Adventure. It's a great place; you should try it."

"Maybe I'd be willing to try the restaurant, but I really don't want to be set up. Thank you for thinking of me, but I'll pass."

Stephanie and my mother pleaded with me a little, but I wasn't having it. How would a restaurant owner have time to take me out anyway? I would think that while I worked days, Monday through Friday, he would have to work nights and weekends.

As the sun started to set, my cousins headed out on the road back to Lawrenceville, and Tex and Stephanie bid us "adieu." I stuck around for a while longer. My father built a fire in his chiminea in the backyard and I pulled up a beach chair near it. He looked at me. "You know, it's only your first couple of weeks back at work. You'll get back into the swing of things and you won't be so stressed. It will all be fine."

"Thanks, Dad, I appreciate that and I appreciate all that you and Mom do for me."

It was chilly outside. I grabbed another glass of wine and wrapped myself in a blanket. The baby was asleep inside with my mom keeping a vigil eye over her. My father brought out some marshmallows to roast. I hadn't roasted marshmallows since I was a kid and they had a way of making me feel like I had traveled back to those days when life was easy. The annual fireworks started. *This is the life*, I thought. *This is what I love about this town. My family and friends, good food, the ocean air, and fireworks*. I felt totally relaxed. I wished every day could be this way.

● ● ●

I was up at five o'clock in the morning, before the baby stirred. I tiptoed to the kitchen and put her bottle in the warmer. I selected a Wild Mountain Blueberry K-Cup. I needed the caffeine today—I was feeling the effects of last night's two glasses of wine. I popped a couple of Tylenol and had barely enough time to finish my coffee when Mandy woke up. I took care of her needs, then showered and dressed. It was getting hot outside so I had selected a gray skirt and a green short-sleeved top to wear today.

I picked up the morning newspaper outside of my front door on the way to drop off Mandy. The Town of Sunshine had hit the headlines again. *"Egg on Her Face"* was the title. I quickly skimmed over the article. Mr. Crazy Eyes was arrested for the egging. I wasn't sure if he was immature or a nut case. I texted Bonnie after I buckled Mandy in her car seat: *Front page, lol.* A few beats later, I got a reply: *I know! What a wacko. Mayor is probably pissed!*

There was a mound of paperwork waiting for me this morning—not only my work, but the administrator's work too. I secretly hoped I wouldn't hear from the mayor today; she was sure to be in a bad mood. I was in the middle of signing purchase orders when I looked down at my shirt. *Crap!* I thought. My breasts were leaking. I didn't have this problem while I was breast-feeding, but now that I was trying to stop, the milk just started leaking out. I wasn't prepared for this. I didn't think to buy any leakage pads to prevent myself from having this mishap. I reached for my tissue box. Empty. *Double crap!* I really needed to start bringing an extra shirt to work. I thought that I could possibly dry my shirt with the hand dryer in the ladies' room for the time being. If not, I would have to run out for an early lunch to change. I folded my arms over my breasts and ran out of the door with my head down. I was walking fast and before I knew it—*crash*. I smacked right into the chest of Officer Williams. I turned bright scarlet. I had never felt more humiliated in my life!

"In a hurry?" he asked.

I mumbled, "Yes," and took off at full speed to the bathroom. I stayed in there, cleaning my shirt and hiding from him until I knew the coast was clear. I did not want to have to explain why my boobs were all wet. He was young and single. I'm sure he never experienced parenthood and I surmised he was clueless about the inner workings of the female breast. He was probably getting quite the laugh at my expense right now. I did my best, drying my shirt with the hand dryer. It didn't look too bad. I padded my bra with toilet paper, then peeked out into the hallway to see if the coast was clear. Through the main doors, I could see that Officer Williams was outside in the parking lot, talking to the mayor. I hurried back into my office before anyone could see me.

Bonnie started on me right away. "Ah, I see you bumped into Mr. Drop-Dead-Gorgeous," she said sarcastically.

"I'm mortified right now."

"I don't think he noticed."

"I hope not!"

"He is a hottie, but there's something about him I don't like."

What? How could there be something about the most perfectly made creature on Earth that she didn't like? I know he didn't talk very much. He wasn't as friendly as Tex, but in my opinion, that made him a little more mysterious and very intriguing. He was the type of guy who could have any woman in the world. I guess I had to admit to myself that I *did* like this guy and certainly wouldn't mind it if he asked me on a date. Because I wanted everyone to think I was okay being a single mom and that I was independent enough to take care of myself, I refused to tell anyone that I didn't want to just date. I wanted a father for my child. And since I seriously doubted he was ready to settle down with a new baby at the moment, I was S. O. L.

"If you don't like him, then why do you keep trying to get me to go out on a date with him?" I asked her.

"I'd simply like to see you get out and enjoy yourself. You are such a great person and I know that what your ex did to you was terrible. You have a full-time job and a second full-time job raising a baby on your own. You deserve some fun. Besides, people don't usually get serious with their rebounds anyway. I never thought you should get into a relationship with him. He doesn't strike me as the relationship type. He's more of a heartbreaker type. I just think you should do him."

"Seriously, Bonnie? I should *do* him? That's not quite my style."

"To each their own, but wouldn't it be nice to get all dressed up, eat a little dinner, sip a little wine, and have someone dote on you for one evening?"

I imagined that would be nice. It would probably be smart for me to take baby steps with someone new instead of jumping right in to a relationship. I wasn't crazy about the idea of dating someone from work. Everyone would talk about us. I'd be embarrassed. Well, not as embarrassed as I was today with my leaky ladies, I suppose.

I was becoming very torn about Officer Williams. I wasn't sure I'd have anything to talk to him about. While I did like the idea of getting out for an evening with a hunk of a guy, I think I liked the fantasy that I had drawn up in my head more than the reality of actually going on a real date. I doubted he'd ask me anyway, which was good. It meant that I wouldn't have to make any decisions about him.

"I wouldn't have anything to wear," I told her.

"I'll take you out shopping. I hate to be the one to tell you this, but you could use a makeover. Plus, I feel bad about the little problem you had today with your ta-tas. You deserve something nice."

"Fine. I'll ask my parents to watch the baby on Saturday. I realize I'm a mess."

"You are a mess, but I'll fix that."

• • •

Saturday couldn't come quickly enough for me. I dropped the baby off in the morning and headed over to Bonnie's Taj Mahal beachfront home. Her house was pale pink this week.

"Did you change the siding since I was here last? I thought your house was yellow. I almost drove right past it."

"I got sick of yellow. My husband hates the pink, but it reminds me of Bermuda's pink sand."

It must be nice to switch your house color on a whim. My house was dark green with burgundy trim. It had been that way forever. I wasn't sure if that was Uncle Lou's choice or if Uncle Lou bought it that way. I certainly didn't have the funds to paint my siding whenever I felt the urge.

I slid into the cushy charcoal leather seats in Bonnie's shiny new black Mercedes. She revved the engine, then pulled out of her three-car garage, making a right onto Beach Boulevard. She made a left onto First Street and headed toward the causeway.

"Where are we going?" I asked.

"I thought I'd take a ride out to Jackson to the outlets since there are a lot of stores there."

"Jackson? We should try that Bratz Restaurant for lunch."

Bonnie was game to try a new place to eat. She merged onto Route 195 and headed west toward Jackson. Within thirty minutes, we were pulling into the outlets. She then dragged me from store to store for hours.

I had to say, Bonnie was a fantastic personal shopper. I should have brought her shopping with me all the time. She had an eye for what would look good on a person's body. She picked out the perfect pair of jeans to fit my shape. I had sticker shock at first. I usually spend around twenty dollars on a pair of jeans. These were eighty-five dollars. I also got a cute peach halter top to match the jeans on a clearance rack for only five bucks.

Bonnie wouldn't let me leave without the perfect little black dress, a more casual sundress, and accessories that could be mixed and matched with what I bought. She said I needed to be prepared for any type of date I went on. Jeans for a sporting event, something fancy for dinner and dancing, and something for a picnic or casual affair. Not that I expected to have a date anytime soon, but at least I had some clothes that fit me that I could wear anywhere, not only on a date. When I couldn't possibly stand another minute because my feet hurt so badly, she agreed to take a break for lunch. We hopped back in the Benz and she sped off to Bratz at around one o'clock.

Bratz was located on County Route 526. A large parking area was placed in front of the restaurant. The façade was red brick with large windows. Their sign was a deep red color. Inside was modern-rustic. The walls were painted copper and had barnyard-looking wood trim. Strangely, it didn't have a country feel to it. There was a large bar area toward the back, which had at least twelve specialty beers on tap and over thirty varieties of bottled German beers.

The hostess escorted us to a booth not too far from the bar area. There was still a decent lunch crowd inside. I looked over the menu.

"Can I get you something to drink?" the waitress said with a large smile. She was dressed like a traditional German beer maiden straight out of Oktoberfest. Bonnie chose one of the bottled German beers. I noticed that they had Woodchuck Hard Cider, so I selected that since I'm not a big beer lover. "I'll give you a few minutes to look over the menu while I get your drinks."

"This is a really cute place," Bonnie said.

"I have a confession to make," I told her. "Tex and his wife were trying to play matchmaker with me and the owner of this place."

"Really? What does he look like?"

"I don't know; I didn't ask. I said I wasn't interested."

"Well, it looks like he does a good business."

The waitress arrived to deliver our drinks and take our order. The menu was very unique. There were twenty-seven types of bratwurst to choose from in two categories: traditional brats and exotic brats. The exotic list included ostrich and pistachio, smocked kangaroo, and smoked alligator. I opted for the chicken, apple, and cinnamon brats. Bonnie chose something more to her caliber of taste buds— the sweet duck and fig with a touch of brandy bratwurst.

"I have a question for you," Bonnie said to the waitress. "Is the owner here today? I'd like to meet him and tell him what a wonderful restaurant this is."

I opened my eyes wide and kicked Bonnie under the table.

"What?! Don't you want to see what he looks like?" she asked.

The waitress responded, "Oh, I'm sorry, he doesn't work weekends. He'll be back on Monday." And she strolled off to the kitchen to place our orders.

Truthfully, I was curious to see what he looked like, but I didn't want him to know who I was, so I wouldn't have been so blunt as to ask for him personally at our table. I felt a twang of disappointment that I couldn't check him out after all. I guess I was wrong about a restaurant owner having to work all weekend.

We finished our delicious meals and headed back to the island. It was nice to have a day out with a friend. I enjoyed myself. It was a much-needed tension reliever.

# 6

*I*t was Thursday night and I was inside the courtroom, setting up for the council meeting. My heart skipped a beat when I saw him. Officer Williams was scheduled to work the metal detector tonight. He waved to me from the back of the room.

"What are you doing here tonight? Where is the guard?" I asked.

"Vacation," he responded.

His blue eyes were dreamy, but I had to snap out of it. It was seven fifteen and the mayor had arrived along with several council members. I was relieved when I switched on the recorder at seven thirty and there was no sign of Mr. Triggers. The mayor called the meeting to order and I did the roll call. The Pledge of Allegiance followed, then the approval of minutes. Still no Triggers in sight. When it was time for public comment, the regulars lined up at the microphone.

First, there was Rose Sciaratta. Rose was in her seventies and as thin as a strand of spaghetti. Her hair was bleached blonde and done up high in a bouffant. Her voice was gruff, probably because she had smoked two packs of cigarettes every day for almost her whole life. She strutted to the podium with her long, slender, wrinkled, fingers holding an opera length cigarette holder.

Mayor O'Donnell spoke up. "Rose, you know you aren't supposed to be smoking in here."

"I swear, doll, I put it out on my way in," Rose said. It was hard to tell if the stench of smoke was emanating from a lit cigarette or Rose's clothing.

Mayor O'Donnell asked her to state her name and address for the record. Rose complained about her landlord. "My slumlord is at it again! The heat is broken in the apartment and he won't do a darn thing about it."

"Rose, it's summertime. Maybe the heat is shut off this time of year and not broken," Mayor O'Donnell informed her.

"No, it's broken! I'm telling you, it's broken!"

"We'll send our inspectors out to take a look tomorrow."

This was pretty much the same thing Rose did at every council meeting—complain about her apartment and her landlord.

Next up was Giuseppe Fruscione, another senior citizen, who complained about the noisy renters next to him. He was an army vet from WWII and had lived in Sunshine his whole life. He was in great shape for being ninety-two years old and he was still very sharp and witty. He always dressed to impress in his suits and bowties. He walked up to the microphone with his cane.

"I need you to do something. These college kids are up all night; they play loud music. They smoke and throw their cigarette butts all over my yard. There are beer bottles all over the place. This is my home and at my age, I deserve some peace and quiet. Isn't there anything you can do?"

The mayor looked toward Officer Williams, who was standing in the back of the room. "Officer Williams, would you please speak to Mr. Fruscione about his noise complaint after the meeting and see if someone is available to do a drive-by tonight?"

"Absolutely, Mayor," Williams responded.

I began to imagine him driving by my house in that sexy uniform, but my fantasy was interrupted by the beeping of the metal detector. I glanced up to see that it was my not-so-favorite resident, Mr. Triggers, walking in before Giuseppe finished his speech. I'm sure I frowned, although I tried to hide it by burying my head in my computer, typing away. He immediately got in line for public comment. *What a jerk,* I thought to myself. He made me go through all that hassle over those boxes, then never bothered coming back to the office to look through them.

Mitchell Looney was the next speaker. He was our resident "pothole police" and he told his tales of where potholes were appearing in our roads. He was probably in his forties and looked like he stepped out of a time machine from nineteen seventy with his long, brown, hippie-like hair. He was the guy who made beer in his bathtub and stayed glued to the TV, watching *Ancient Aliens* all day long.

"Um, yeah, I was walking in front of the ice cream shop on the corner of Thirteenth Street and I noticed a pothole there. Someone could blow out a tire. Would you mind having someone go out there and take a look at it?"

"Sure thing, Mitch. We will send public works out to take care of that," the mayor replied.

Mr. Triggers stood up to the microphone next. Once again, he preached about the dunes. The mayor interrupted him. "Mr. Triggers, we have already told you we cannot help you with the dunes."

Mr. Triggers turned red. "You are a stupid louse and all this red tape is bull. You are such a moron to think you can't do anything. It would only take fifteen cents per resident to bring over a few loads of sand to put at the end of my street. So here is your fifteen cents, you cheap bitch!" He reached in his pocket and threw fifteen pennies at the mayor.

Mayor O'Donnell started banging the gavel wildly. She was furious. "Officer! Officer!" she screamed, calling for Williams. "Remove Mr. Triggers, I want him arrested!"

What happened next was somewhat of a tornado. I guess Williams called for backup and when Mr. Triggers would not leave peacefully, he and another officer tackled him to the ground. Mr. Triggers was kicking and shouting, "I want my dunes, I want my dunes!" Chairs went flying, papers were scattered throughout the room, and audience members scrambled out of the way. I ducked behind the dais—I didn't want to get hit in the eye with any stray pennies or police bullets, for that matter.

The mayor adjourned the meeting and I was left to clean up the mess. *Tomorrow's another day,* I thought and I went to my car to drive home. On my way there, I chuckled at the recollection of what happened. I mean, it wasn't funny at the time, but it sure seemed funny now.

The next day, I decided to drop off Mandy a few minutes early so that I could stop at Take Ten, the only coffee shop in Sunshine. I love their sugar-free, fat-free chai latte. For some reason, it always made me feel calm and peaceful. When I arrived at work, I went straight over to the courtroom to clean up the mess. A few minutes into repositioning the toppled chairs, Triggers appeared at the clerk's office window. Bonnie came to get me.

"Mr. Triggers is at the window and he's asking for you," she said.

The tranquil effects of my chai suddenly wore off. I cringed. *Wasn't he in jail?* I thought for sure he was arrested last night after they took him out in handcuffs. I knew he was going to take up a good amount of my time, so I told her to tell him that I was in a meeting and that he was welcome to look through the boxes. Bonnie came back a few minutes later. "He doesn't want to look through the boxes; he wants to see you personally," she said.

"Tell him I'm not available at the moment and ask him if he'd like to make an appointment," I said.

I finished cleaning up the room and putting the chairs back in order. Thirty minutes later, I headed back to my desk. To my dismay, Triggers was right there at the counter waiting for me. *This is someone who doesn't have a life,* I thought. He was dressed head to toe in banana yellow, including his socks and the bandana he had wrapped around his forehead. Bonnie could not say his clothes were mismatched today. The song "Mellow Yellow" started playing in my head. The yellow part was right, but the mellow part didn't quite fit Mr. Triggers.

"How may I help you?" I asked him.

First, Triggers told me he didn't have time to look through the boxes today and that he would be back on another day to look through them. The thought of my having to deal with him coming back on another day made me ill. I was also annoyed that I also had to continue to deal with the boxes all over the place.

Then, Triggers handed me a list of documents that he wanted copies of, such as flood hazard maps and house elevation standards. Bonnie and I took out the materials and provided the copies he wanted. Then, he handed me a request for sand dune management plans. I copied those for him. Then, he handed me another request for various purchase orders. When I returned with the purchase orders, I had to inform him that one year was destroyed in accordance with State laws. This bit of news did not sit well with Triggers. I showed him the permission slips I had obtained regarding the destruction of the documents. After scowling at me, he started with a barrage of questioning.

"Who made the decision to destroy the purchase orders? Was it your finance division or that stupid mayor herself? Why would you destroy them? I don't understand why you would destroy them. They take up so little space. There is no reason for you to destroy such small documents. This is a perfect example of government red tape. Preventing the public from finding out what is really going on around here."

He rattled off the questions so fast that I didn't have time to answer them. Clearly, he did not want to hear any explanation. It wasn't our policy to keep records past their retention periods; it had nothing to do with preventing the public from obtaining information. To him, it might seem like a small file folder containing only the purchase orders he requested. To me, it was one folder, then another folder, then another, which amounted to twenty boxes per year that had to be stored somewhere. Plus, when you actually counted up all the purchase orders from all the departments of the town, there were hundreds of them yearly; not quite the small amount that Mr. Triggers thought. Since there was no storage here in our small municipal complex, the town had to pay for storage. It wasn't financially wise to keep dozens and dozens of extra boxes around when we typically didn't have requests for older records like this.

"I know you are either hiding something or you're an idiot!" Triggers shouted at me.

"Mr. Triggers, I can assure you that I am not hiding anything. I am only doing my job."

I didn't address the idiot comment. I felt it wasn't worth it. He was possibly the most annoying person I had ever encountered in my life. I used to think Mitchell Looney with his pothole complaints at every council meeting was the most annoying person I knew. Triggers changed all that. I had a theory—Mr. Triggers was put on this Earth in order to make Mitchell Looney seem normal. Normal people would fill out one form, listing all the documents they wanted, then leave it with me so that I could compile everything. Normal people didn't hand me one list, then a second, then a third, fourth, or fifth. Normal people didn't demand that I wait on them for hours at a time. Normal people understood the meaning of the word *no*. Triggers was anything but normal.

After an hour and a half of berating me, he finally left. I could feel the tension releasing from my shoulders the second he walked out. I hadn't noticed that Tex had come in through the back of the office while Triggers was here.

"Having trouble?" he asked.

"What do you think?" I asked, sarcastically.

"Aw, but I thought for sure he brought the sunshine to Sunshine today with that outfit."

"Yeah, the outfit was a little bright, but his personality…not so much," Bonnie said.

"Seriously, wasn't he arrested last night? Why was he here?" I asked.

"He was arrested," Tex said.

"Then why isn't he in jail?"

"He was released on his own recognizance."

Bonnie chimed in, "What was he arrested for? Assault with deadly loose change?"

"Disorderly conduct," Tex said.

"Well, what if he comes in here throwing things around, like his big rock?" I asked. "What if he hits one of us? Would that be assault? Would that keep him in jail longer?"

Tex shook his head at me and said condescendingly, "Next time he comes in here, pick up the phone and dial 9-1-1 if you feel threatened at all. We are right across the parking lot."

"That doesn't make us feel any better," I said, annoyed.

"And I checked out the rock thing. It was one of those plastic fake rocks to hide a key in."

"Oh. Then why did he bring it in here?"

"How the hell should I know?"

I hustled back to work. I was behind in my meeting follow up since Triggers took up all my time this morning. After an hour went by, I was so engrossed in paperwork, I didn't notice it at first. But then I heard it....*drip, drip, drip.*

*What the F?* I thought. *Oh well, I'm too busy to deal with whatever that is right now. Back to advertising ordinances.*

*Drip, drip, drip.*

I called out, "Bonnie, is that getting louder or is that my imagination?"

*Drip, drip, drip, drip, drip.*

Bonnie said, "Yeah, where is that coming from?"

I stepped outside my office into the space where Bonnie sat and looked around. It took me a few minutes, but there it was—the ceiling was leaking.

"Where is the water coming from? It didn't rain. Do you think the air conditioning is broken?"

Bonnie looked at me blankly and shrugged.

I bent over to get a garbage can to collect the dripping water and I heard a loud crack. I gasped. Gallons of water burst through the ceiling tiles and landed on my head and back with a huge splash. I was soaked.

Bonnie burst out in laughter. She was laughing so hard that tears were streaming down her face. I just stood there in the huge puddle with my eyes wide, mouth opened, and hair plastered to my head. I was dripping from everywhere.

I suddenly heard laughter from outside of our counter area. Oh no! It was Officer Gorgeous walking by, witnessing the mess. Could I be any more embarrassed in front of this man? When Bonnie saw him, she laughed that much harder. I felt the sudden urge to beat her over the head with Mr. Trigger's pet rock. I was frowning at her and cursing her in my head when all of a sudden...*crash*! More water smashed through the ceiling tiles, landed on Bonnie's head, and kept gushing. She jumped out of the way, but not before she was soaked through all her clothes as well. She stopped chuckling, but I couldn't control my laughter at this point.

"My shoes!" she screamed.

Of course, Bonnie would be worried about her shoes.

"They are Cesare Paciotti's and I just got them on sale! Seven hundred dollars right down the drain! They're ruined!" She started to cry, but those were no longer tears of laughter.

I guess I'd be a little upset too if I had paid seven hundred dollars for my shoes. Fortunately, I got them for thirty bucks at the outlets and I was pretty sure the water wouldn't affect them. What I was more worried about was the damage to our records and our office. I ran outside into the lobby to check on the boxes. Those boxes contained permanent records and I was hoping they hadn't gotten wet.

Luck was on my side. The boxes were dry. I inspected the ceiling for signs of a leak, but couldn't see anything. I silently cursed Mr. Triggers again for having me bring boxes over. I was going to be really pissed off if anything happened to them. I placed garbage cans under each of the drips and called the public works department in a panic for help.

Public works arrived with wet vacs and buckets. They brought over tarps to cover the boxes and equipment, and crates to use as a base for the boxes in case the leak spread to the hallway. The mechanic headed upstairs with his tools. The rest of the guys started sopping up the water in our office. I closed the window to our office, then Bonnie and I headed home to change.

• • •

First thing Monday morning, I pushed through the doors to the municipal building and noticed it was like the Heat Miser's lair. Tex was already waiting in my office.

"Oh boy," I said. "Why do I not think this is not a friendly visit? You only seem to come around anymore when there is trouble."

"I hate to be the bearer of bad news, but it appears that you had the flood because someone tinkered with the HVAC system. And when I say tinker, I mean that they did so much damage, that it's irreparable."

"Do we know who did this?"

"I'm going to need a list from you of everyone you can remember who was in the building last week."

"Oh geez! That is going to be a long list. I probably won't remember the names of the residents who came in, unless they paid for something, then I would have a receipt. Triggers was in on Friday, an hour before the flood. Then there was the council meeting last Thursday. All the meeting regulars were there—Rose Sciaratta, Giuseppe Fruscione, and Mitchell Looney. The mayor and council. Me. Officer Williams working the metal detector. Triggers came to the meeting late. I'll ask the other departments to compile lists as well."

I was glad that Rodney would be back to work later this week. I was tired of dealing with crazy stuff getting flung on me. I called public works and asked them to bring over as many fans as they had for all the offices in the building. I opened up all the windows and I began a quick inventory around the office of anything that might have gotten wet. The copier seemed to work. The rugs were dry now, thanks to public works, and the computers were booting up. I saw there was a pile of papers that got wet, but I could reprint those documents. The fax machine was dead. I checked inside the file cabinets, and discovered the water didn't leak inside. Looked like we got lucky again.

Next on my to-do list was informing the powers-that-be about the issues here. However, that would have to wait; the fire alarms were ringing.

"Rats," I said.

"You've only been putting up with this for a few weeks. I've been dealing with this since March. I have nightmares about alarms," Bonnie said.

"Hasn't anyone contacted the alarm company to get it fixed?"

"Repeatedly."

"This is like the boy who cried 'wolf.' One of these days it's going to be a real fire and no one's going to believe it."

Out to the parking lot we traipsed. When the first firefighter jumped off the truck, Bonnie whispered in my ear, "I'd like to slide down *his* pole."

I shook my head at her. "There is something wrong with you."

"Now how could you say that? I'm the only person standing outside here that knows how to find something positive about having to stop what I'm doing and stand outside in the blazing heat."

"I think it's hotter inside; people are probably content to be out here right now."

"You are so negative."

Ten minutes later, we were back to work. I picked up the phone and dialed the mayor to see what she wanted to do about replacing the HVAC system.

"Good morning, Mayor O'Donnell. It's Chelsey."

"Hi, Chelsey, how are you?"

"Well, not so great. Remember how I told you about the air conditioner causing the flood on Friday? Well, Detective Texidoro was here and he said it was tampered with and that it's not able to be fixed. Our next meeting is a week from Thursday. Do you want me to get some quotes and do a resolution for that meeting?"

"Yes, that would be fine. Was there anything else you needed for the flooding? Was any equipment damaged?

"Surprisingly, the equipment all seems to be working, except for the fax machine. I have some money in my budget to get an inexpensive one. Public works did a good job of getting rid of the water. The carpeting looks better than it did; I think they cleaned it. I'm not sure if any mold will surface in the upcoming days. I don't know how long the system was leaking before the water came through. I will put through an insurance claim today."

The insurance company wasn't liking us too much these days. All we had were claims. Fires, robberies, and floods. I usually didn't have to deal with insurance issues, but with Rodney out, that suddenly became my job.

"What about your records; do you need any kind of records recovery service?" Mayor O'Donnell asked.

"No, we're okay. The papers that got wet are all in the computer and we can reprint those. The boxes in the lobby for Mr. Triggers were untouched. Everything that was inside the filing cabinets seems to be fine."

"Thanks, Chelsey."

I told her I would review everything with Rodney when he returned this week and we disconnected. I also made the decision to write an email to Mr. Triggers and tell him he had one more week to come in to review the documents in the boxes, otherwise they were going back into storage.

# 7

*A*nother Thursday night, another meeting. I was in the courtroom setting up as usual and feeling grateful that public works had been able to jerry-rig the air conditioning until a new system could be installed. Mr. Triggers arrived early and I was thankful that the guard was there so that I wasn't alone with him. He had never responded to me about the boxes going back into storage. I was afraid he would come over and yell at me. The green plaid necktie on his white button-down shirt almost looked normal until you saw that he completed his look with jean shorts, black socks pulled up to his knees, and white sneakers. I thought Bonnie was being kind when she said he was an "eccentric" dresser.

Within a few minutes, Giuseppe Fruscione arrived with a plump, juicy tomato in hand for me.

"Really? For me? I can't take that from you."

"Chelsey," he said, "I know how much you say that you like Jersey tomatoes! This is from my garden. You know it's hard to grow these in this sandy soil, so I grow them in a container. Besides, my tomatoes are the best; you take it home and enjoy it."

"Mr. Fruscione, how can I thank you?"

"No thanks are necessary!"

Yum. I *do* love Jersey tomatoes. I was looking forward to lunch tomorrow. A nice cheese and tomato sandwich with mayo. Homegrown Jersey tomatoes don't taste like store-bought tomatoes. They are so much more flavorful.

My thoughts were broken by the sound of the gavel. The mayor was calling the meeting to order.

Mr. Triggers was first up when the public comment period was called. I saw Rose Sciaratta take out her cigarettes and head toward the door. I guess she figured this was going to take a while.

"Mayor O'Donnell, I'm here to ask if you are going to put the dunes up at the end of my street," Mr. Triggers said.

Mayor O'Donnell replied frankly, "We are not installing dunes, Mr. Triggers."

At that moment, Mr. Triggers reminded me of a cartoon devil, with his dark eyes and how his neck and face flared up into a bright red color. All he was missing were horns.

Triggers raised his voice. "Well, since you look so much like a man, why don't you grow a pair of balls under that skirt of yours to go along with your penis and put those dunes in place?"

Mayor O'Donnell shrieked and before I could think, she grabbed the tomato that Giuseppe gave me and threw it at Triggers. Triggers ducked and the tomato flew straight across the room, hitting Rose square in the head. She dropped her cigarette inside before she tumbled out the half open door. The cigarette landed on the pile of agendas and *poof!* Up they went in flames. The fire alarms were triggered and the noise was so ear piercing that it was hard to think. The guard grabbed the fire extinguisher and put out the flames, but not before the room filled with smoke and damage was done to the walls and carpeting.

I covered my mouth and nose with my shirt and escaped out of the emergency exit that was close to my seat. I jumped into my car to move it before the fire trucks arrived and blocked me in. I wasn't sure if I was more upset about the fire or the fact that I would be missing out on my cheese and tomato sandwich. I wondered why I ever decided to come back to work instead of being a stay-at-home mom. Oh yeah, that's right, I needed the money.

● ● ●

The next morning, I arrived early to work. Rodney had previously sent out an office memo that we were having a potluck lunch today for all the staff. With so many things happening, I initially thought it was a good idea on his part. We all needed some morale boosting and this might do the trick. Now, with having the fire in the courtroom last night, I wished he had scheduled it for a different day because I had too much going on.

I pulled open one of the front doors of the municipal building single-handed, while juggling my crock-pot in my other hand. I had made my famous root beer pulled pork. Bonnie offered to get the rolls.

I headed to the kitchen and searched for an electric outlet. I had to fire up the crock-pot so that the pork would be ready in time for lunch. As I bent over to plug it in behind the table, I heard a familiar voice. I slowly stood up and turned around. A twinge of humiliation combined with a rush of blood to my heart made my cheeks flush. *Oh no!* I thought. *Officer Gorgeous just got a full view of my big ass.*

"Officer Williams. How nice to see you. What are you doing here so early?"

"I brought the lasagna over from the PD for today's lunch to put in the fridge."

"Oh, I love lasagna. Well, see you."

I darted out of the kitchen, then slapped myself mentally on the forehead. Why couldn't I think of anything better to say than "Oh, I love lasagna"? I am such a dork. My mind went totally blank when he was around. Why didn't I ask him something about himself? I could have gotten to know him better. *All right, get a grip,* I told myself. *I have a baby at home, I've got a full-time job, I started working out again. I have no time in my life to sit down for thirty minutes and watch a rerun of* Friends; *I certainly do not have enough time for a man!*

I headed to the courtroom to assess the damage. It had a smoky stench. Public works was already there, ripping out the carpet and airing out the room. They told me it wasn't as bad as it looked. It was just cosmetic.

I trotted back to my office. Bonnie had just arrived. "What the hell happened here last night?" she asked.

She must have noticed the courtroom. I started to laugh uncontrollably. Bonnie couldn't understand a word I was saying because I was hysterical.

"What? What tomato? What the heck?" she asked.

When I finally regained my composure, I gave her the gist of the story. "Giuseppe Fruscione brought me a tomato. Triggers said something nuts to the mayor. Mayor O'Donnell threw the tomato at Triggers. He ducked, Rose Sciaratta got hit in the head, dropped her cigarette, and set the place on fire."

"Holy shit! At least the fire alarms worked this time," Bonnie exclaimed.

We both chuckled.

"You have to listen to the audio of the meeting later. It's crazy, but right now we have a lot to get done before lunch today," I said.

We buried ourselves in paperwork. I felt like every time I accomplished something, something new popped up for me to finish.

When the clock read eleven forty-five a.m., I got up from my chair to go check on the pulled pork. As I headed out to the kitchen, I noticed Mr. Triggers walking in, but I was pretty sure he didn't see me. I wasn't in the mood for him today. I stepped into the kitchen, grabbed a fork, and lifted the lid of the crock-pot. As I stirred in a little more barbeque sauce, I inhaled the steam. It smelled good and I was so hungry. I thought about eating a sandwich before the crowd got there, but I thought I'd better wait another fifteen minutes.

I took my time walking back to my office in hopes that Triggers would be gone by the time I got there. No such luck. I found him arguing with Bonnie at the counter to our office. I stepped into the office and locked the door behind me. I didn't want to be in the same area with him without a

77

barrier between us if I could help it. I noticed that Mr. Triggers could stand to be introduced to deodorant.

"Mr. Triggers, how can I help you?"

"Hey moron! I want to speak to the mayor!" he shouted.

"I'm sorry, Mr. Triggers, the mayor is only part-time and does not have an office here. I could take your phone number and have her call you."

I could hear Bonnie under her breath saying she already told him that.

"I want to talk to the mayor, now!" Triggers yelled impatiently.

"The mayor is not here," I answered.

"Do you work for the mayor?" he asked and before I could answer, he started firing a range of other questions at me.

"Why isn't the mayor here? Doesn't the mayor have office hours to speak with residents? Doesn't the mayor think it's important to be here for the residents?"

I tried to make a mental note of the questions, so I could answer them. I said, "Well, I…"

He cut me off. He pointed at me and yelled, "I am not done talking, moron!"

I usually pride myself on being helpful, but it was clear to me that this insulting guy did not want answers to his questions. He wanted to speak with the mayor and he was not going to be patient about it. He said that I didn't understand why he wanted to meet with the mayor and he started on a forty-five-minute exposé about his life, his house, and the dunes he wanted. Obviously, he didn't remember that I was well aware of the situation. I suspected he was older than I originally surmised and I wondered if he was losing his mind, his memory, or both.

Each time I tried to get a word in, he would get angry and cut me off. I had learned along the way that sometimes an irate customer just wants to be heard and doesn't really want a solution to their problems. So I listened. And listened. And listened. Then my mind drifted, imagining the food in the kitchen. My stomach was grumbling. I could smell the food. I could see the various employees heading over to the kitchen and closing their offices for the lunch hour. I was jealous. I was annoyed. I was wishing he would go away. Then finally, he stopped talking.

I snapped out of my daydream. I did not know what else to say other than what I had already said to him, so I asked, "Would you like me to have the mayor call you to set up an appointment?"

"No, I want to talk to someone immediately."

"I'm sorry. I don't know Mayor O'Donnell's schedule and I don't know when she will be in. I can call her for you and ask."

"Yes, I want you to call her now."

Oh great. I had forgotten the mayor wasn't around. She had left this morning on vacation to Florida to visit her family and I really did not want to bother her. Plus, she didn't typically answer her phone when she was out of state. I told him I would get her number and call her and I headed into my office to make the call. As I predicted, there was no answer.

I came back out to the counter after a few minutes and informed Triggers that I had left a message.

Triggers persisted. I tried to reassure him that I would call him as soon as I heard something, but he kept at me. My head was spinning. I was starving. I suddenly felt nauseous—I sometimes get low blood sugar when I haven't eaten. I didn't know what to do. Maybe I needed a man to tell him the same thing I had been telling him. Mr. Triggers seemed not to like women too much. I mean, everyone liked Bonnie—she was super sweet to all the residents, but he hated her.

"Let me see what I can do, Mr. Triggers. I will get the administrator and be right back."

I pulled Rodney away from the party and asked him please to talk to Mr. Triggers for me. It was one o'clock and the party was wrapping up anyway. Rodney seemed very calm today and he smelled like the men's cologne counter at Macy's. I wondered if he had been smoking a little sumthin' sumthin' before work and was hiding the smell with his friend, Tommy Hilfiger.

Rodney approached Mr. Triggers. He reminded me of a used car salesman in the way he spoke. He was very slick. He had Triggers smoothed over and out the door within twenty minutes. I hadn't noticed that Bonnie had returned. She could see the look of pure frustration on my face.

"Do you want me to run out and get you something to eat? Most of the food is gone, although there may be some dessert left."

I told Bonnie that it was not necessary for her to run out for me, I would leave for lunch now. I was famished and starting to feel faint. I wished I had eaten breakfast that morning, but I thought there would be an absurd amount of food at lunch. The one cup of coffee that I had this morning was the only thing keeping me going. Why didn't I just eat that sandwich when I was checking on the pork earlier? I had to stop being so polite!

I hustled into the kitchen to grab something to hold me over until I could buy some food. I was pleasantly surprised when I found the plate of homemade chocolate cookies in the fridge. It looked as if someone had forgotten to take them out.

I quickly unwrapped the plastic wrap and shoved one in my mouth. *Oh my. This is orgasmic,* I thought. *I have to get this recipe.* I took three more cookies. I thought to myself, *this is why I can't lose that last ten pounds of baby weight. I do nothing but eat junk food these days.* I shoved another cookie in my mouth. It was mouthwatering. It was soft and delicious. Simply euphoric! I took a bite out of the third cookie.

I started to calm down from my Mr. Triggers fiasco. I mean, who did he think he was? I started to smile. The whole thing was pretty funny though. The way he threw his change at the mayor, the way he came in all demanding. I started to giggle. I know they say chocolate has some chemical reaction in the brain, the same reaction that love has on a person, and wow…whoever said that is on to something. I giggled some more.

I looked up to see Bonnie come strolling in the kitchen and then I saw the immediate look of horror on her face.

"Oh my gosh! Please do not tell me you ate those cookies!"

I giggled at her. She looked so serious. "Why? Were they made with laxatives or something?" I joked with her.

She yelled at me, "Rodney made them!"

Oh no. I threw the partially eaten cookie on the floor and jumped away from it. I spit out what I was chewing in a napkin. I wasn't feeling good from the chocolate. I was feeling good from the dope! Oh, no. A million things went through my mind. *Should I go to the ladies' room and make myself vomit? I've never been high before. Is this what it feels like? Oh no, how am I going to take care of the baby? How am I going to drive?* I thought Rodney only made pot brownies. How was I supposed to know he also made "feel good" cookies? How the heck was I going to explain this to my parents? *Oh wait, I'm old enough. I don't have to explain this to my parents.*

My train of thought was broken by Bonnie saying, "Have you ever been high before?"

I guessed she could see the concern written on my face, or maybe she just knew me by now.

"Don't worry," she said. "I doubt you are feeling the effects if you've never tried marijuana before."

I heard her calling my parents and telling them that I wasn't feeling well and saying she would take me home. She asked them to keep the baby overnight because I didn't want Mandy to catch my stomach bug. She marched me back into my office, handed me my cell phone and purse, and took my car keys. She said she'd drive me home in my car and have someone pick her up to bring her back to the office. She told me to sleep it off and that I'd feel normal again in the morning. I started to giggle.

"What is so funny about this?" she asked.

"I was thinking…I guess this is absolutely what you would call a 'pot' luck lunch!" I burst into laughter.

"I'm glad you still have your sense of humor about you."

"Am I going to get arrested for taking an illegal substance? Or lose my job?" I asked Bonnie.

"You're not going to tell anyone," she said.

# 8

Sizzling was the best way to describe August this year. We were in a drought and conserving water. Luckily, residents hadn't complained about it; no one had a lawn to keep green in this town. I was pleased that our HVAC system was replaced and no one had tampered with the new one.

Rodney appeared at the our office window at three o'clock. "You two can go ahead and close up early. We're closing down the building for a day or two."

"Why?" I asked.

"The mayor said she saw a bedbug and she wants it checked out by an exterminator. She didn't want any of the employees to have to be in the building if there are bedbugs in here."

"Well, I should hope not."

Bonnie looked at me like she was going to throw up. "If there are bedbugs in here, I'm really going to freak out."

"I know. That's disgusting. Let's get the heck out of here," I said.

I closed the office faster than I had ever closed it before. I grabbed my purse and ran to my car. I was completely repulsed. I entered my house through the backdoor, which was adjacent to the laundry area. I stripped off my clothes and threw them in the dryer with my shoes on the hottest setting to kill any traces of bedbugs or their eggs. I then hopped into a hot shower. Knowing there was a possibility of nearly invisible little creatures crawling on my body sent chills down my spine. I shampooed my hair four times and scrubbed my skin twice.

I threw my hair in a ponytail since I didn't feel like drying it, put on some new clothes, and headed over to my parents' house to get my daughter.

The building remained closed for another day while it was fumigated. It was Friday when we were able to return to work. While I didn't feel like going back to work for fear of bedbugs, the agenda was due for the council meeting and I was already behind due to having off yesterday. I put a fake smile on my face, hiked my purse onto my shoulder, and walked through the main doors to start my day.

"It smells in here," Bonnie said.

"Would you rather have bedbugs in here?" I asked.

We saw Rodney walking by in the hallway. He had a giddy look on his face and his cheeks were a little red.

"Someone's been smoking the green stuff," Bonnie said.

"*Shhh*! He'll hear you."

I went to the hallway and followed Rodney. "Rod, how did you make out with the exterminators?"

"Just fine," he said. "They said they couldn't find any evidence that bedbugs were in here, but they sprayed just in case."

"That's a relief," I said.

I reported the news to Bonnie. "No bedbugs were found; they sprayed as a precaution."

"Is this stuff safe for us to inhale? It's really stinky."

"Open up some windows. I'm sure the smell will air out."

Just then, the fire alarms roared.

"Better yet, you can get some fresh air outside," I said to Bonnie.

We stood under a tree in the parking lot to stay as cool as we could from the heat. We watched Engine No. One pull into the lot.

"Over here, Mr. Fireman. I got a fire burning right here," Bonnie said as she made a hand motion toward her "personal space."

"You are going to get into so much trouble if someone hears you," I told her.

Bonnie smirked. "I hope it's the good kind of trouble."

"I am going to walk away from you now."

"Oh, lord. Why are you so prissy? I'm just joking. They are all the way over there with the engine rumbling. No one can hear me but you."

I rolled my eyes. Not only was she going to get herself into deep water one day, she was going to get me into trouble too since I was her boss and witness to her sexual bantering.

I looked to my right and saw Mr. Triggers pulling into the parking lot.

"Ugh, not again," I said. He had already been here twice this week and I really did not feel like dealing with him for a third time. He was wearing orange shorts, a pale blue polo that was too small for his large belly and a green necktie. He saw Bonnie and me standing under the tree and approached us.

"Hello, Mr. Triggers," I said. I gagged on the odor coming from him. Bonnie cupped her hand over her nose nonchalantly, like she had an itch, and she turned in the opposite direction. I tried to breathe through my mouth.

Triggers handed me a nine-page records request, then left.

"Thank god he left right away," Bonnie said. "I almost puked in my mouth."

"Do you think he just doesn't shower, or do you think he doesn't wear deodorant?" I asked.

"I don't know and don't care. I'd rather smell the pesticides in the office than his stink any day."

"Agreed."

"You would think his wife would tell him he stinks."

"He's married? I find that hard to believe."

"He wears a wedding ring."

"I never noticed. Poor woman. I guess that goes to show there's someone for everyone."

"What the hell is he requesting now?" Bonnie asked

"Nine pages of junk, let's see..." I started to read down the list of demands. "Ethics forms for all employees, the coastal hazard mitigation manual, construction permits for those who have elevated their houses, the dune revegetation program, the beach protection plan, the name and address of the mayor's full-time job, so on, and so forth."

"Sounds like he's targeting the mayor."

"I know, right? If I were her, I'd hire a security guard."

"Are you going to give him her job information?" Bonnie asked. "If I were the mayor, I wouldn't want him to know where I worked. He might start showing up there like a stalker."

"Good point. I don't know if I have to. I'll have to look for a law about whether or not that is considered confidential information. I might be able to deny it on the basis that it is a request for information and not a request for a particular document. But, he's going to figure it out anyway, you have to list your source of income on the mandatory ethics forms. The name of her job will be listed on her ethics form, and he could just look up the address on the internet."

I never gave Mr. Triggers the information on the mayor's full-time job, but I heard from the mayor that he had indeed figured out where she worked. He showed up at her work several times, harassing her. She had to file a formal complaint with the police department. They gave him a warning that he was not to show up there again.

• • •

The next week, Triggers stopped in to see me Monday, Tuesday, and Wednesday, two hours each day. He was either picking up records or requesting more of them. He was usually angry. He never smiled. He always insulted me. He was especially annoyed whenever I had to tell him I couldn't disclose something.

The second I thought to myself that I couldn't take him any longer, that I couldn't keep up with all my work and spend fourteen hours per week on one resident, he took a break from his visits to the municipal building.

On Monday, August 13th, Bonnie and I came to work prepared to go through everything in our office in an attempt to find the missing safety paper. Between Triggers, break-ins, floods, and fires, I hadn't had much time to stop and look through everything, but I knew this had to get done.

I was dressed in jeans and a short-sleeved navy blue blouse. Bonnie wore jeans with three-inch heels that probably cost more than my entire wardrobe combined. She had on a fancy multi-colored shirt and she was adorned with lots of jewelry. She looked more like she was going out clubbing than going through papers in an office.

"Did you, by chance, box up any records while I was on leave?" I asked her.

"No, I didn't have time to do that," she said.

"Did it possibly end up in the trash by accident?"

"I guess anything is possible. I was beside myself, insanely busy with work, while you were gone, but I honestly don't think it would have ended up in the trash. I typically don't take the pack of paper out of the drawer. Whenever I get a request, I pull out only the amount of paper that I need—a few sheets at a time at most."

"What about when the FBI agents were here? Do you think they had a reason to take it?"

"It's possible."

"First thing we need to do is go through everything in this office—every storage cabinet, every drawer, every file—to see if we misplaced it. If we still can't find it, I'll get in touch with Tex to see if he can find out if the Feds took it. If we don't have any luck there, then I'll have to notify the state registrar. I hope it's not missing because that would be a hassle for us. They will probably tell us to stop issuing certified copies until they investigate."

I saw out of the corner of my eye that the mayor was waiting impatiently at the door to our office.

I let her in, saying, "I'm sorry, Mayor, I didn't see you standing there."

"No worries, what were you saying about safety paper?" she asked.

"Oh, I guess I haven't told you that around the time of the break-in, we noticed some safety paper was missing. I'm not sure if it was taken at that time or perhaps misplaced. We are doing a thorough search of the office today and if we don't find it, we'll take the next steps."

"Have you already reported the paper missing?" she asked.

"I did report it to Detective Texidoro previously—when he took my statement after the robbery. And he knows that we are not sure if it was taken during the robbery or if we simply misplaced it. I'll notify him of my findings tomorrow, then I'll email the state registrar to let him know what is going on."

"Okay," the mayor said with a strange look on her face, and then she left.

"Do you think she's mad about something?" I asked Bonnie.

"That was a weird look she gave you," Bonnie responded.

"Maybe she thinks I took too long to look into this? Or maybe she's worried something bad is going to come of this?"

"Maybe a bug crawled up her rectum and bit her."

We both laughed and shrugged it off as we resumed our search for the paper. A few moments later, the fire alarms went off again.

"I'm really sick of this," I said to Bonnie.

"You think you're sick of it, I've been putting up with it since you were out on maternity leave."

"I don't understand why they don't get it fixed. Battery-operated smoke detectors would be better than this."

We headed out of the office to wait in the sweltering heat. The fire trucks rolled up to the building and Bonnie spouted her inappropriateness like always.

"Oh, Mr. Fireman, come on over here and let me see your big apparatus."

"Oh, puh-lease!" I said to her as I chuckled.

We were dripping with sweat by the time they allowed us back into the building.

"Those firemen make me all hot and bothered," Bonnie said.

"You better watch that your husband doesn't hear you talking about firemen in your sleep," I said.

We continued our search for the paper. After seven hours of hunting, we gave up. We looked in every file, every drawer, and every crevice of office space, but we didn't find the paper.

"Looks like we need to see if the FBI took the safety paper. I'll make a note to call Tex in the morning. He probably has a contact and could find out for us. I know he's not on duty today," I said to Bonnie.

# 9

The next day, I arrived at work to find Bonnie busy typing the meeting minutes from the last council meeting. She was wearing a dress that was charcoal with sparkles on the bottom and crinkled silver on top. I suppose that was the latest fashion, but I thought she looked a lot like Jiffy Pop. I suddenly had a craving for popcorn. She had her earphones on and she must have forgotten that no one could hear her when she started to bop her head and rap.

"What are you singing?"

She didn't hear me. I stood at her desk and waved in her face. She took out the earphones. "What are you singing?"

"Oh...well, I was thinking that I could make a rap album from our meeting regulars and sell it for lots of money."

"What?"

"Let's take Rose, for instance," she said as she broke out into song, *"My slumlord's at it again, my slumlord's at it again...my slumlord, my slumlord, my slumlord's at it again."*

I couldn't control myself. I found this hysterical. "Do Mitchell," I said.

*"I'm gonna blow out a tire, there's a pothole in the road. I'm gonna blow out a tire, a tire, a tire. There's a pothole, a pothole, a pothole,"* she sang.

"Giuseppe?"

*"The renters are loud, the renters are loud…the renters, the renters, the renters are loud."*

"Triggers?"

*"You got the red tape, you got the red tape, I need my dunes, and you got the red tape."*

"We can call the album, *Sunshine Rapping.*"

We were laughing so hard, I almost missed Mr. Cutie walking by. He waved.

"Hello, ladies!"

"Hi, Officer Williams," I said.

I snapped out of my momentary dream world and turned to Bonnie. "Speaking of Mr. Triggers, can you believe he wasn't at the last meeting? What's that all about? I think he's up to something."

"Yeah, that's strange. He hasn't missed any council meetings since he started coming to them. Maybe he woke up and got himself a life."

I went into my office to get some work done. My mind was filled with questions of what could have happened with the safety paper. I was about to make the phone call to Tex when I heard Bonnie. "Oh no! You son-of-a-bitch!"

"What? What's wrong?"

"This freaking computer! I typed that whole set of meeting minutes. Three freaking hours of my listening to these crazy people talking and the damn thing didn't save."

I looked at my own computer screen and saw an error message: *Your network connections have been lost.*

"I'll call our computer IT company and see what's up," I said to Bonnie. I picked up the phone to dial the help desk.

"Phones are out too," I told Bonnie.

I reached into my purse and pulled out my cell phone. I wasn't sure if the two problems were interrelated, but I opted to call the computer company first. The man on the other end of the phone said that from his end, it appeared the server was disconnected. He asked me to go see if it was turned on. I went down the elevator to the basement to see what was going on in the server room. All the lights were on and everything looked normal to me, which wasn't saying much. I didn't know a thing about computer servers. I went back upstairs and reported my findings. They told me they would send out a tech to look at it today.

"See, I told you Triggers was up to something," I said jokingly to Bonnie. "Didn't you tell me he was a retired computer tech? He probably spent the last couple of weeks learning how to get into our computers and mess up your meeting minutes."

"No, I told you he was in a biotech field," Bonnie explained.

"Oh, my bad."

"Bye, ladies!" I heard Officer Williams say.

"Bye, Mike," I called out.

"Oh, are you on a first name basis with him now?" Bonnie asked me mockingly.

"Oh lord, don't start with me. Sometimes I call him by his first name; depends on my mood."

"I know what your mood is."

"What?"

"Hot and horny. When was the last time you did it, anyway?"

"None of your business, that's when."

"*Hmm*, let me guess…the baby is around seven months old now and you were pregnant for nine months…"

"Knock it off, Bonnie."

"I'm just saying…you're stressed out and a little game of hide the sausage would do you wonders."

"*Eww*, did you seriously say that? I should fire you."

"You love me; you'd never fire me."

True. I'd never fire her. She was a dedicated and loyal employee. She was meticulous with her work. It was hard to find good help, so I overlooked most of her inappropriate comments. Plus, she put a smile on my face.

"Since you can't type meeting minutes now, why don't you head down to Rodney's office and find out if anyone reported the phones not working?" I asked.

She threw down her pen and hustled out of the office. I called over to the police station from my cell phone. The non-emergency number wasn't working. Bonnie came back and reported that Verizon was sending out a tech to look at the phones. I told Bonnie I was heading over to the police department to talk to Tex.

I took my cell phone with me and walked across the parking lot. I approached the dispatch window and asked if Detective Texidoro was in today. The dispatcher said he was, then he buzzed me through. I headed back to the detective area to find Tex in his office.

"Desk duty today?" I asked him.

"Yeah, I'm trying to catch up with everything. What's up?"

"When the FBI raided the municipal building this year, did they leave behind a list of records that they took from my office?"

"I have a copy of something; let me go get it. But before I do that—why are you asking?"

"Remember I told you about that missing safety paper? We haven't come across it yet and I wanted to make sure the Feds didn't take it before I notified the New Jersey State Registrar of Vital Statistics."

Tex left the room and came back with some papers in his hand. He said, "I don't see it listed here on the log of what they took, but I have a contact phone number if you want that."

"Please and thank you," I said.

He handed me the phone number and I turned to leave, but I remembered something.

"By the way, did you get the fingerprint results yet?" I asked Tex.

"Yes, they were inconclusive. The perp or perps probably wore gloves both during the robbery and while tampering with the HVAC system."

"Do you think it's Mr. Triggers? The man always seems to be around when something goes haywire."

"We are investigating that."

I headed back to my office. I asked Bonnie if anything was working yet. She said, "No."

I picked up my cell phone and dialed the number Tex gave me. It was for Special Agent Salvatore Romeo. I got his voice mail, so I left him a message explaining why I was calling.

I felt a little lost with no computer, no email, and no phone. It was like being back in the Dark Ages. I had become so accustomed to working with all the new technology, there wasn't much for me to do. I started to review the agenda items for Friday's deadline.

It took several hours, but finally, the computer and phone companies arrived on site to fix our issues. By four thirty, they were still working on the problems, so I left for the day.

Later that evening, I had put Mandy to bed and was enjoying a glass of white wine when my cell phone buzzed. It was a number I didn't recognize.

"Hello," I answered.

"Ms. Alton? This is Special Agent Salvatore Romeo. You had left me a message earlier today. I'd like to meet with you confidentially. When do you think you'd be able to set up an appointment?"

"I guess next week will be fine."

"I'll contact you again with a firm date and time."

"Wait, before you hang up, I believe I should notify the state registrar about the safety paper. Do you have it?"

"We do not have it and that is why I'd like to meet with you."

"Okay, thanks. Should I go forward and report the paper missing?"

"Yes. We can bring the state registrar up to speed next week as well."

"Okay, thanks, bye," I said. The phone disconnected. *Gee,* I thought, *he didn't even say goodbye.* It sounded to me like he knew something about the safety paper. I wondered if that was what the raid was about last April. Perhaps the safety paper was stolen and not missing.

I stayed awake half the night. It was like a hamster was in my head, running on his wheel, and I couldn't fall asleep with my mind spinning.

What reasons would someone want to steal safety paper? To create a fake ID? I wondered if any of our younger employees, those under twenty-one, would be taking the paper so that they could go out drinking. Were there any illegal immigrants working for the town, who needed to fake their birth certificates? Since you have to be a US citizen to work for our town, that idea wasn't plausible. Was anyone selling IDs for money?

I noted a list of suspects in my head. Bonnie? I didn't see what incentive Bonnie would have to take the paper. She certainly didn't need money. Rodney? Maybe he needed money. He had missed a lot of work and with all his medical bills—that could be a possibility. Mr. Triggers? Besides the break-in, I didn't see how he would have had access to our office, unless the office was broken into back before April. Unlikely, though. I think the locked fireproof cabinet where the paper was kept would have been damaged. The exterminators? Nope, the paper was missing before then.

I decided to keep my thoughts to myself. I didn't want to go around wrongly accusing anyone with my wild ideas. I wanted to wait to talk to the FBI to see what their take was.

# 10

It was hump day and it was nice to be halfway through the week already. I walked in to work to find Rodney having a conversation with the mayor. They were saying something about the phones lines being slashed and computer hacked into. Keeping my big mouth shut would have probably been a good idea, but something came over me and I couldn't control myself.

"Are you freaking kidding me? Something else was tampered with? Do either of you even care about our safety? This is the third incident since I've been back from leave. Fourth incident if you count the fire last March. What is it going to take for you people to do something, like put in a decent alarm system? It's bad enough that the fire alarms go off every week! When is that going to be fixed? And maybe the public shouldn't have access to areas like the phone room and computer room. How about putting up some cameras? Are you going to wait for someone to be held at gunpoint before you get moving? I know government is historically slow, but this is ridiculous. We shouldn't have to work under these conditions."

I stomped back over to the clerk's office and slammed the door behind me. Bonnie could tell I was furious.

"What's wrong?" Bonnie asked.

"This place is pissing me off," I said. "Someone messed with the computers and phones; they didn't malfunction by accident."

"You're kidding me."

"No, I'm not, and I just gave Rodney and the mayor a piece of my mind. Maybe if Mr. High-as-a-Kite came back down to Earth once in a while, we'd have some security measures in place. We are the ones that have to deal with all the problems—cleaning up after floods and robberies, not being able to get our work done. I don't feel safe working here anymore."

"The police are right across the street."

"Yeah, and if someone came in here with a gun, they would blow our heads off before the police put down their donuts."

"Get up on the wrong side of the bed this morning?"

Maybe I was in a mood. Perhaps it was PMS, sleep deprivation, or the stress from work. Was it the anxiety over the upcoming FBI interview or a little bit of all of the above? I started to think I never should have left my job as a deputy clerk in another town. There was no drama there. No foul play. No crazy residents. If I were there, my boss would be handling everything and I'd just be doing my work, collecting a paycheck.

"I'm sorry; I'm in a mood. Wasn't your anniversary yesterday?"

"Yup," Bonnie said.

"I am so sorry I forgot. Happy anniversary!"

"Thank you!"

"Did you do anything special?"

"Well…let me start by saying, I got my dreams fulfilled."

"Oh really? How? Did Jayce buy you something nice?"

"Not exactly. Let's just say I got a gorgeous firefighter to show up at my door and rescue me in my bedroom."

"What are you talking about? You didn't cheat on Jayce, did you?"

"No. The kids were at a sleepover, so I decided to plan a romantic evening for Jayce. I went out and bought a very expensive red lace negligee with matching thong lace panties."

"Do I want to hear this story?" I said sarcastically.

"Are you going to let me finish?" Bonnie asked, then she continued. "I placed rose petals all over the bed and lit red candles to set the mood."

"I can almost see where this is going."

"No, you can't. Now stop interrupting. Where was I? Oh yeah, so Jayce took one look at me in that sexy nighty, and he threw me down on the bed, ripped off my panties, and started making mad passionate love to me. I'm not sure when it happened, but all the banging must have made one of the candles fall onto the floor. I noticed flames going up the curtains, and smoke. I screamed and ran into the bathroom to get water. I only had a cup, so I filled it up with water from the sink and threw it at the flames, then ran back a couple more times to get more water. Jayce ran into the bathroom to try to help and he slipped on the water that I had dripped onto the floor. His feet flew out from under him and he cracked his head on the tile floor. He was just lying there, bare naked, with his head bleeding."

"What did you do?"

"I did what any dedicated wife would do. I admired his hot body for a beat, then remembered I should call 9-1-1."

"Oh, my god," I said, trying to hold back my laughter. "Did they show up when you were naked?"

"No, silly, I threw on a robe."

"What about Jayce?"

"Oh, I threw a washcloth over his privates."

"Was he conscious?"

"Sort of…well, not really. He was a little out of it. I think he had a concussion."

"Did the EMTs know what the two of you were in the middle of when the fire started?"

"I'm not sure, but who cares if they did? I mean, we're married. People have to expect that we do the deed sometimes."

"What about the fire?"

"Oh, I think I put it out before the firefighters got there, but it was still smoldering, so my dream guy came in and shot the curtains with a fire extinguisher. I was awful tempted to take off my robe and thank him."

"Oh lord, you are too much! Did Jayce go to the hospital?"

"No, I think he was too embarrassed since he works there. He refused treatment. Told them he was a doctor and he knew he'd be fine."

"Do you have a lot of damage to the house?"

"Not really. I have a contractor there today, fixing it up as good as new. I wanted to redecorate anyway."

"Bonnie, I have to tell you, that has got to be the funniest story I've heard in a long time. The EMTs were probably laughing at you two all weekend."

"I know, it was pretty darn funny!"

I plopped down in the chair at my desk. I was much calmer now. Bonnie had a way of making me smile. I booted up my computer and saw that we were back up and running. I didn't think to ask this morning during my tirade if everything was fixed. I started to think about contacting the state registrar. The current registrar was a man named Charles Alfred. I didn't know him personally, but I had heard him speak once at a seminar. It was nearly impossible to get in touch with him. He was dealing with over five hundred towns at any given time on the phone, so I opted for an email message. I knew he quickly responded to email.

I told him that it had come to my attention that some of our safety paper was missing. I provided him with the sequential numbers of the sheets I presumed were gone. I informed him that the FBI was aware of the situation and would probably like to speak with him. I asked for further instruction.

Within a nanosecond, I received a reply: *You have reached the NJ Department of Health, Bureau of Vital Statistics and Registration. The Bureau will be closed from August Thirteenth through August 31*<sup>st</sup> *on furlough. We appreciate your email and we will reply on or about September 4*<sup>th</sup>.

I heard a knock on the edge of my open office door. It was the mayor. I suddenly felt warm around the collar, wondering if I was going to get reprimanded for my little outburst this morning.

"You can come in," I said.

She came in and sat at the chair opposite my desk. "Chelsey, I know you are under a lot of stress. I assure you, in next year's budget, we will look into additional safety precautions. We spent a lot of money on the new HVAC system and we don't have money to spare to address the other issues. It's not in the budget at the moment for security cameras, or to hire an employee to stand guard at metal detectors into the building. For the time being, the police are on alert and they will be patrolling this building more frequently. We are hoping the police catch the criminal or criminals and the problems will not reoccur. Meanwhile, if you can come up with any suggestions for safety that we may have overlooked, please let me know."

"Other towns have swipe cards to enter and exit the building and office areas. They record who has been in and out, and the time. Perhaps if we had those, we would be able to tell if any employees were involved," I told her.

"Okay, we can certainly look into that. Why don't you research the costs and provide me with an estimate. Anything else?"

"How about a panic button for our office?"

"We may be able to do that now. I'll ask the police chief to tell me how difficult that is."

"That would make me feel a little safer, but I sincerely hope you give careful consideration to getting a new alarm system now and not waiting for another year. You could purchase a system now as an emergency, then fund it in next year's budget. If you are planning on paying for it next year anyway, then it shouldn't matter if you install it immediately."

"Okay, Chelsey. I will ask Rodney to research that. Meanwhile, how did you make out with the safety paper?"

I told her that I tried to contact someone at the State, but apparently, they have been placed on a furlough until Labor Day, so I would have to wait until September to talk to them. I purposely omitted the information about my upcoming meeting with the FBI. I worried that she would tell someone, who would tell someone else. I feared the news would get back to someone it shouldn't.

The mayor said, "I know our budget is tight this year, but at least we didn't have to furlough our employees like the State did to make ends meet." She stood up to leave my office, but turned back and looked at me one last time. "You look exhausted," she said, "I think you should take a mental health day tomorrow. Go home, relax, get some sleep. We'll see you on Friday."

Fine by me. I hadn't taken a day off since I had been back from maternity leave and I was happy to have some extra time to spend with Mandy. I was also quite relieved that I didn't get reamed out by the mayor. She turned out to be much more understanding than I gave her credit for.

I finished up my work and at four thirty, I packed up my desk, and told Bonnie I wouldn't be in tomorrow.

I drove to my parents' house and stayed for dinner as usual. I couldn't cook like my parents did. In reality, it's not that I *couldn't* cook, it's that I didn't *want* to cook. Slaving over a hot stove would take away time that I wanted to spend with my daughter, so I gave up cooking. When Mandy became old enough to participate, then I'd start cooking again.

My mother didn't work while I was growing up, so she had time to both cook and spend time with me. I remembered the days we would be rolling out dough and making cookies. I wished I had the luxury of being a stay-at-home mom so that I could share those experiences with my daughter daily. I never thought I would say that. I always loved to work and until recently, I loved my job. I still had a passion for being a municipal clerk, but I was feeling burnt out working in Crazy Crime Land with Mr. Crazy Eyes Red Tape bugging me for months. I was also missing Mandy. I know I saw her every day, but it didn't feel like it was enough.

My parents worried about me. It was their wish that I would have been married to a wonderful man by now. A man who would take care of me so they didn't have to feel like I was still their responsibility. I wanted that for myself too, but life didn't work out that way for me. I felt guilty leaning on them so much. They were my anchors and I was grateful that I had them both in my life. They were extremely attached to Mandy too, so it wasn't all bad. I suppose I was feeling a little sorry for myself.

• • •

I went back to work, after having off for a day feeling refreshed, even though it was a Friday and it was likely going to be tedious. There was lots of paperwork to complete because it was the deadline day for the council meeting agenda. Everyone submitted their requests at the last possible minute, as usual. Being out of the office yesterday didn't help matters. My desk looked like a typhoon hit it. I had over twenty items left to prepare for next week's meeting and I didn't know how I was going to get it all done. I heard a man's voice at the window. "Chelsey Alton, please."

Bonnie came in my office and informed me that a sheriff's officer was asking for me. I walked up to the window.

"Hi, I'm Chelsey. May I help you?"

"Are you Chelsey Alton?"

"Yes."

"You have been served."

He handed me a package and asked me to sign a document certifying that I had received the lawsuit. It wasn't as bad as it sounded. It was the town getting sued, not me personally. Just another one of my many job duties—to receive service for the municipality. I tore open the envelope and chuckled. Mr. Triggers was suing the town.

"What is it?" Bonnie asked.

"A lawsuit from Mr. Triggers."

"Regarding the dunes?"

"Yuppers."

"Now you know what he was up to."

"Yeah, maybe that's why he hasn't been around. He was busy preparing his legal briefs with his attorney."

I scanned the document and forwarded it via email to Mr. Betts and our insurance carrier. I wasn't sure which one of them would be the defense attorney. When it's a bigger case, Mr. Betts typically handles it. For smaller cases and tort claims, it's typically the insurance company. I guessed they worked it out amongst themselves as to who would take on the case.

I shot an email over to the mayor and council as well, informing them that we had been served. I got back to work and finalized the agenda for approval by the mayor. Then I worked on drafting the remaining agenda items and waited on several customers in between.

"Hey, Bonnie, that last guy that came in paid with a one hundred-dollar bill. I'm going to run to the bank on my way home to cash it."

"All right, see you on Monday."

I stayed late to finish everything and I noticed Officer Williams in the building when I left.

"I see they've stepped up patrols in this building like the mayor told me they would," I said to him.

"Yup," Officer Williams said as he quickly left.

I was beginning to think Bonnie was onto something with this guy, about how she said there was something about him she didn't like. Some days he was friendly and outgoing. Other days he was short and cold with me. His personality seemed to change with whatever direction the wind was blowing. I was hoping I'd get to talk to him a little more, but I chalked it up to him having something of importance on his mind.

I left the municipal building and, without thinking, I turned in the wrong direction. I was dog-tired and momentarily forgot that I was heading to the bank, which was in the opposite direction. I swung onto Twelfth Street and headed up to Beach Boulevard to turn back toward the bank. As I drove toward Fourth Street, I saw a creepy man with a picket sign in the middle of the road. Cars were passing by, beeping at him.

"You have got to be kidding me," I said out loud to myself. It was Mr. Triggers walking back and forth in front of Bill Bradford's house with a sign that said, "We want dunes! Give us dunes!"

I pulled out my cell and dialed the police non-emergency line.

"Sunshine Police, Dispatcher Forty-one," could be heard through my car's Bluetooth speakers.

"Hi. This is Chelsey Alton, the Town Clerk. I know people have a right to peacefully protest, but do they also have the right to block the middle of a street?" I asked.

"We'll send someone right out."

I gave the dispatcher the location and swerved around Mr. Triggers. A thought flashed across my mind—I could have run him over and put an end one of my problems, but I wasn't sure if anyone was looking out of their windows. Plus, I didn't want any of his bloody body parts stuck to my bumper. I also knew the police were on their way and the last thing I needed was to go to jail over some loser.

I stopped at the bank, changed the hundred-dollar bill, then went on my way to my parents' house to pick up Mandy. I opted to drive down Main Street and avoid the possible police scene and Mr. Triggers. Mandy was sound asleep when I got there.

"I have a chicken casserole in the oven," my mother promptly announced.

I stayed for dinner and filled my parents in on the today's antics of Mr. Triggers. Mom and Dad were good listeners. I think they enjoyed the drama. All of my recent work-related stories were nothing short of a soap opera.

We finished eating just as Mandy woke up, so I loaded her in the car and headed out for home. After I put her down to bed, I headed out to the living room with a glass of white wine and a good book. Before I knew it, it was five o'clock in the morning and I realized I had fallen asleep on the couch.

# 11

By eight thirty on Monday morning, I was walking through the doors to the municipal building. Outside of my office were Tex, Officer Williams, Bonnie, and Rodney. I thought, *Oh great! What is going on now? Another break-in?*

"What's up?" I asked. Officer Williams piped up, "Chelsey Alton, you are under arrest."

"WHAT?" I shouted. "For what?"

"Theft and embezzlement."

I looked at Bonnie with a look of both confusion and shock. Bonnie was biting her nails and shaking a bit. "They said they saw you steal one hundred dollars out of the cash box. I told them you were only making change."

"You have got to be kidding me," I said. "The money is right in my purse; it's all there in the bank envelope. I took a one hundred-dollar bill to the bank last night to get smaller bills."

"Put your hands behind your back," Officer Williams said as he put his hand on my shoulder and turned me around. "You have the right to remain silent..."

"Tex?" I said with a tear in my eye.

"Chelsey, don't worry, we will get this all straightened out," he responded.

I noticed an audience in the hallway. Everyone had come out to see what the fuss was about. Officer Williams cuffed me. I started crying.

"Bonnie, please call my parents."

I was beyond humiliated. With everyone I worked with watching, I was marched over to the police station in handcuffs, fingerprinted, and put in a locked cell. I could not stop the flow of tears streaming from my eyes. I didn't understand. I had always made change when we had a large bill. I couldn't fathom why there was an issue this time. It's not like I had forgotten to bring the money back. This whole thing was ridiculous.

After a few hours, Tex finally came in to see me. My eyes were swollen and inflamed from all the crying.

"Chelsey, I can't tell you what is going on exactly, I mean, this is a criminal investigation, so I'm limited as to what I can say. The only thing I can do is say don't worry, this will all be taken care of."

"Don't worry? You want me not to worry? How can I not worry? I didn't steal that money! I didn't do anything wrong! I have a baby at home; how can I not worry?"

"Do you trust me?"

"Yes."

"Good, then you are going to just have to trust me on this one. It will all work out; everything will be fine. I'm on your side, but don't talk to anyone from the town. You need to watch your back."

I didn't understand how he could say that everything would be fine. He wasn't the one locked up here in this filthy two by four cage. He wasn't the one who had to spend money on an attorney for no reason. And who was I watching my back from? Was someone out to get me?

"Do my parents know?" I asked him.

"They do and they are going to come get you."

Five hours later, I heard the buzz of someone being let into the lock-down area. "Chelsey Alton, bail's been posted." I felt slightly comforted, knowing I would be out of jail soon. I was escorted into the processing area, where I signed some papers, then I was moved into the lobby, where I saw my dad waiting. I started to cry again and he gave me a huge hug.

"We know you didn't do this, Chelsey. Jose explained everything to us. I'm going to take you to your house to pick up the things you need, and you are staying with us tonight."

"Thanks, Dad," was all I could muster between the sobs.

Back at my house, I grabbed some clothes and toiletries, along with all the items Mandy needed for an overnight stay. My father drove me over to the municipal building to retrieve my car. Dinner was on the table at my parents' house when we arrived, but I didn't have much of an appetite. I learned that my parents had put their home up as collateral in order to bond me out. I felt sick to my stomach.

The next morning, I arrived at work, as usual, to be greeted by Rodney. "Chelsey, please come into my office," he said. I walked down the hall into his office, where he closed the door.

"I'm really sorry to have to do this to you, Chelsey, but I have to put you on administrative leave."

"What happened to innocent until proven guilty?" I asked.

"I'm sorry, but Officer Williams said he saw you taking the hundred dollars, and then you admitted to it being in your belongings."

"This is ridiculous, Rodney. You know that I always take large bills to the bank to make change. You know that we can't make change for the following day if I don't break the large bills. I cannot believe this is happening. Is this paid or unpaid leave?"

He looked scared to tell me. After a few seconds, he responded, "Unpaid and yes, I know you make change, but Williams said you left work traveling in the opposite direction of the town's bank."

*Great,* I thought. *Now I have no job and no income because of some giant misunderstanding.* I wondered if it would make a difference if they knew I made a wrong turn.

"The fact that I phoned dispatch after I left work to tell them that Mr. Triggers was in the middle of the road with picket signs on Fourth Street should be an indication that I was in the vicinity of the bank last night."

"You'll have to tell that to the judge."

"Fine," I said and I got up and opened the door. There was Officer Williams, waiting for me. Great, just great. I turned back to Rodney, "What? You didn't think I'd leave peacefully? Believe me, I don't want to be here as much as you don't want me here." And I left with Officer Williams at my heels.

"Chelsey, do you need anything from your office before you go?" he asked. He almost sounded like he felt sorry for me. I gazed into his big blue eyes. "I know you're only doing your job, but this is awful for me and I'd just like to go directly to my car."

I certainly didn't want to talk to him, the man accusing me of stealing money. Why wouldn't he simply ask me about it instead of immediately arresting me? He walked me out to my car and I drove back to my parents' house.

When I got there, I picked up the phone and called the Municipal Clerk's Association of New Jersey. I was a member of the Association and luckily, I had been paying into their legal defense fund. I knew they would be able to help me out.

They recommended an attorney and said they would mail me forms to fill out for partial reimbursement of my attorney's fees. I was thankful that they had offered such a service; otherwise, I don't think I would have been able to afford a decent attorney. I also didn't know any attorneys who specialized in this sort of thing.

My next phone call was to the lawyer, Gary Schubert. Mr. Schubert's secretary set up an appointment for me for the next day. Unfortunately, his office was located over an hour away in Hamilton Township. It was too difficult to find an attorney nearby that didn't have ties to the town or county and would be able to represent me without it being a conflict of interest.

When I finally got off the phone, my parents asked what happened. I burst into tears, sobbing hysterically. "I got fired," I said.

"They can't fire you," my dad said. "You haven't been found guilty of anything."

"Okay, not fired; put on 'administrative leave' without pay. I might as well be fired."

"Did you find a good attorney?"

"I have a meeting with one tomorrow."

"We'll watch Mandy for you tonight and tomorrow. You go home, take a nice hot bath, and have a few glasses of wine. You'll feel better after speaking with the attorney."

I put my and Mandy's dirty clothes in a bag, threw my purse over my shoulder, then headed for home. I wanted to get out of Dodge because the thought of Sunshine made me too upset.

• • •

Gary Schubert's office was difficult to find. He didn't have a sign out front. I drove past the building four times before I found it. It was in an older office building with beige stucco siding. I parked in the tiny lot and entered a small landing area with stairs going up and down. I read the sign, which indicated there were two offices upstairs housing a dentist and a realtor. There were three offices downstairs—an accountant, an acupuncturist, and Mr. Schubert.

I climbed down the stairs and pushed open the small wooden door at the end of the hallway, which said, *"Gary Schubert, Esq."* The office was modest inside. A desk was situated facing the door. A closed interior office door was behind the desk area. The office was equipped with a computer, printer, fax machine, copier, and multiple file cabinets. There was a dorm-sized refrigerator in the back left corner with a small microwave sitting on top. No-frills is how I would describe this lawyer.

A chunky, middle-aged lady, wearing black vintage cat eyeglasses and her hair in a bun, asked if she could help me. "I have an appointment with Mr. Schubert," I said softly.

"Have a seat; he'll be right with you," she said. She pointed toward the chairs facing her desk to the left of the doorway. The wooden chairs looked as old as the building and had tattered, burnt orange seat and back coverings. I waited for ten minutes, then Mr. Schubert appeared from behind the closed door.

"Sorry," he said. "You must be Chelsey. I was on a conference call. Please come in and have a seat."

I entered his office, which had barely enough room for a desk and two chairs. I pegged him to be around fifty years old. He had light brown hair and a small brown moustache. He was an average height and size. He wore brown pants and a three-button beige suit jacket. His white button-down shirt was accented with a brown multi-colored tie. His clothes weren't expensive, but he was neat and clean. He looked professional.

I sat across from him. I explained how I was arrested and put on administrative leave. I told him about how I always took money to the bank to make change and that none of this made sense since it was never a problem in the past. I informed him that I was told by the previous municipal clerk during my first week on the job that I would have to make bank runs for change.

He carefully wrote everything down. "What reason did they give for the arrest?" Mr. Schubert asked.

"Theft and embezzlement."

"Interesting. There is no separate embezzlement law in New Jersey. The arresting officer said this to you?"

"Yes."

"I will get copies of the arrest record and other documents I might need from the Town of Sunshine myself so that you don't have to contact them."

"Thanks, I appreciate that."

"Here is the situation. Theft of one hundred dollars is a misdemeanor charge—a disorderly person's offense. It holds a sentencing of restitution, a fine of up to one thousand dollars, and imprisonment up to six months. The major problem you will have with being found guilty is finding a job anywhere. You will have a criminal record for at least five years. This can certainly affect your life in a negative way."

My stomach sank. "Six months in jail isn't a major problem?"

"So long as you don't have a previous criminal record, the judge may waive the jail sentence, which is typical for first-time offenders. You will likely be fired from your current employment, you will have a difficult time finding a new job, and you will lose the right to vote."

"I don't have any previous record."

"After five years, we could apply for an expungement of your record."

I started to tear up. "Five years?"

Mr. Schubert handed me a tissue and continued, "They have to prove two things. First, that you took the money unlawfully and second, that you took it with the intent of not giving it back. The fact that you admitted that you had the money makes it easy for the prosecutor to prove that the money was moved from its original location. The judge may draw an inference that you took it unlawfully. But, if you have witnesses testifying that your intent was to make change and bring it back, then I think we have a pretty good case."

I gave him Bonnie's, Rodney's and Tex's full names and contact information. All of them could vouch that I periodically did bank runs to change large bills, although, I wondered if Rodney *would* vouch for me. Mr. Schubert asked how he could get in touch with the previous municipal clerk. I knew she had moved, possibly to North Carolina, I thought. He said he would try to locate her.

"I have another question," I said. "You said something about the judge inferring I took the money illegally. Won't the jury have to decide?"

"No. If you weren't accused of taking anything more than one hundred dollars, it's not an indictable offense. The case doesn't rise to the level of being presented to a jury."

Mr. Schubert asked if I thought anyone had something to gain by having me arrested or if anyone had a vendetta against me. I told him how Tex told me to watch my back, but I couldn't think of anything or anyone myself. He prepped me for what to say in the event anyone, like the press, contacted me. He thoroughly explained the process that I would be going through and that he would try to get the court to schedule a date as soon as possible.

"Do you think you will be able to get the charges dropped?" I asked him.

"It depends. I'll know more once I question your witnesses and see the police report. Don't worry. I'm good at my job," he said.

I handed him a check to cover the retainer fee. He said he would let me know when he used up the retainer and that he would bill me an hourly rate. He offered to let me pay over a period of time.

I left his office not feeling any less apprehensive. My dad was wrong. I didn't feel better after talking to the attorney. I decided to take the back roads home. I drove from Hamilton Township, making my way through Robbinsville, and hopped onto Route 539 in Allentown Borough. I found myself subconsciously driving to Laurita Winery in New Egypt.

Laurita Winery was a place I had been before. It was nestled back in the woods behind rolling hills of vines. From the moment you turn into their driveway, you get a special feeling—like you've stepped out of New Jersey and into California Wine Country. The tasting room is part of a huge building that has a deli area, a store, a banquet area, and a loft overlooking the entire place. A large, double-sided fireplace divides the banquet room from the tasting room.

I paid the seven dollars for a tasting of six of their wines, then decided on a bottle *Relaxing Red* and a bottle of *Chocolate Therapy* to take home with me. Since the talk with the attorney didn't ease my stress as I had hoped, I knew the wine would. At least temporarily anyway.

I called my parents from my cell phone on my way back home and filled them in on what happened at the attorney's office. I told them I would swing by and pick up Mandy when I got back and head home. They offered to give me the night off instead. I called Bonnie and asked her if she wanted to come over for a drink.

A half hour later, I met Bonnie at my place. We opened up the *Relaxing Red* and had a seat on the couch.

"How did it go with the attorney?" Bonnie asked.

"Not as well as I would have liked."

"Why? What did he say?"

"That I could go to jail."

"Really? That's ridiculous. The money was accounted for."

"He said he'll know more once he gets the police report and he talks to my witnesses. I gave him your name; I hope you don't mind."

"Not at all!"

"I'm scared."

"Don't be scared. Just take this time to spend with your daughter and don't worry about anything else."

"I don't know if I can pay my bills being out on leave this way and having to pay an attorney. I spent my savings when I was out on maternity leave to pay for baby items and bills."

"I have money; how much do you need?"

"Bonnie, I am *not* taking your money!"

"And why the hell not?"

"Look, I really appreciate the offer. It was so incredibly generous of you. I can borrow some from my parents if I really get in a bind."

"The offer still stands if you change your mind."

'Thanks, Bonnie."

We opened the second bottle of wine. I was already tipsy. The *Chocolate Therapy* was like drinking a dessert. My problems seemed to disappear as the wine disappeared. I was two sheets to the wind when we finished the bottle. Bonnie called Jayce for a ride home. I went to bed and passed out.

# 12

*A* couple of days later, a knock at the door roused me from my sleep. Mandy was down for her nap and I used that time to get some much-needed shuteye. I was still reeling from my arrest and I was none too pleased when I looked through the peephole to see two men flashing badges. I thought about not answering, until I heard one of them say, "Chelsey, it's the FBI."

I suddenly remembered that they had wanted to talk to me about the safety paper. They never called me back to set up a meeting time, so I was surprised by their visit. I threw on a robe and opened the door. I was a mess. My hair was like a bird's nest and I was in my sweats. I let them in and asked them to be quiet since the baby was asleep. I told them to have a seat and that I'd be back in a jiffy. I brushed my hair back into a ponytail, brushed my teeth, and quickly slapped on some makeup. I threw on a clean pair of jeans and shirt, then met them in the living room.

They introduced themselves as Special Agent Romeo and Special Agent Lincoln. Romeo was middle-aged, tall, and thin. He had dark hair and dark eyes. He was clearly Italian, with a stereotypical Italian schnoz. Lincoln was thirty-something, African-American, tall and handsome with a nice body. I suspected women fell all over him. They were both dressed in black suits with black ties.

I shook Lincoln's hand first and said, "Are you related to Abraham?" The man didn't crack a smile. *Not in a joking mood,* I thought. I didn't bother to ask his first name. I turned toward Romeo and shook his hand saying, "It's nice to put a face with the name."

"We'd like you to come with us for some questioning," Romeo said.

I could feel my shoulders tense up and my nerves starting to rattle. "I'd love to, except I have a sleeping baby in the other room, so unless you can give me some notice to find a babysitter, then you'll have to talk to me here." I was terrified they were going to take me away and stick me in another jail cell.

They looked at each other like they were not expecting my snippy response. I guessed they didn't do a thorough investigation of me, because if they had, they would have known I was a single mom.

"That's fine," Romeo said. "We can interview you here. We will be recording this interview."

"For quality control assurance?" I asked. I received in return a deadpan stare. Okay, clearly *not* the joking types.

"I want to be clear about one thing," I said. "I wish to know if I am I under arrest again. If so, I want my attorney here and I'm not saying another word until I have him here."

"Again?" Romeo asked.

"Boy, you Feds don't do your research, do you? This wouldn't be the first time this week that a handsome man arrested me. I was arrested on Monday, accused of taking money which I did not take. So, I'm not in the mood for any games or accusations. I just want my attorney," I said defensively.

They looked at each other again.

"What is that secret look for?" I demanded.

"Chelsey, we are not here because you are under arrest. You are not being investigated. This interview is voluntary at this time. If we needed you formally at a later date, you would be subpoenaed as a witness for court," Lincoln said.

"We can certainly schedule a time to speak with you with your attorney present if that makes you more comfortable," Romeo said.

"If you didn't know I was arrested and told not to come back to work, how did you know you'd find me at home?"

"We didn't know you'd be at home. We drove by and saw a car in the driveway, so we knocked. We were going to try your work next if you were not here. We drove from Trenton and this was the first stop on the way," Lincoln explained.

I relaxed a little. They wanted me as a witness and not as a conspirator for a crime that I didn't commit. I could deal with that. They started to ask me about the safety paper. When did I notice it was missing? How many pages were gone? Did I suspect anyone? They asked me a lot of questions about Mayor O'Donnell too. I tried not to sound like a disgruntled employee with a vendetta, but I doubted I was successful.

I got the feeling they already knew the answers to the questions they were asking. It felt like a test to see if I would tell the truth. I wondered why they didn't strap me to a lie-detector machine. The interrogation was stressful. I felt like I was on trial. I told them everything I knew, including that the local police were investigating various crimes that might or might not be connected to the missing paper.

Within an hour, Mandy woke up and started crying. I excused myself to tend to her. When I returned, the agents said they had enough information and would contact me if they needed more.

I asked them, "What does the mayor have to do with all this? Does she have something to do with the missing safety paper?"

They gave each other *that* look again. "We are not at liberty to discuss the details of this investigation with you," Romeo said.

I secretly wondered if I was on to something. Was that the reason I got fired? I showed Romeo and Lincoln out of the front door, then called my attorney to tell him about the interview and my suspicions.

As soon as I hung up with Mr. Schubert, I noticed I had a missed call from Bonnie. I quickly dialed her back.

"Hey, Bonnie, it's Chelsey," I said.

"Well, first it's you, then it's me," Bonnie said.

"What?"

"The mayor made a move to abolish my position. I was laid off today."

I was shocked. "What the hell? Who is running the office?"

"A woman by the name of Lorraine Paso, a friend of the mayor's. She doesn't know her rear end from a hole in the ground. Ugly bitch too, I might add. If I had to take a guess, my guess would be that she used to be a man. A man who had his male appendage circumcised all the way up to his behind. She has a voice deeper than my husband's. Oh, wait, if she had her penis circumcised up to her backside, would her voice be high instead of low? I take it back. My guess would be that she's a woman taking male hormones in preparation of her sex-change operation."

She made me laugh and I needed that. I was in a state of depression, trying to figure out how I was going to pay all my bills.

"What reason did they give for laying you off?" I asked.

"They told me budget cuts, but you and I both know it's because I said I was going to be a witness at your trial, in your defense. I have a feeling there is much more to it than that, though. These politicians have a way of double-talking and blaming everything on the budget when there is actually an underlying agenda. I may not know what their agenda is right now, but you bet your bottom I'll find out what it is, then I'll sue them for wrongful termination for every dime I can get."

I suspected something more was going on also, but I had no way to confirm my hunch. "Do you really think it's because you are going to stand up for me in court?"

"I think that's part of it, although, I can't prove anything just yet. Let's go to lunch. I need a drink. Can your parents watch Mandy for you?"

I left Mandy at my parents' house and headed over to Bonnie's place. I made sure my seatbelt was on, and that I drove the exact speed limit. I didn't want to get pulled over by any of Sunshine's men in blue. They'd probably arrest me again.

We chose Woody's Ocean Grill in Sea Bright for lunch. It was close enough to be a convenient drive, but far enough away where we weren't at risk of running into anyone associated with Sunshine. Woody's had great food and I was dying for their signature drink, an Orange Crush.

A lot of the travelers had left yesterday. Surprisingly, traffic wasn't terrible like it normally was on a Friday during the summer. The weather was perfect out—warm and not too humid. There was one parking space left in Woody's small lot.

We were seated at a booth across from the bar. I ordered the chicken tortilla soup and fish tacos. Bonnie chose the mahi-mahi.

"First things first," I said. "I want to know if you heard about Mr. Triggers and his picket signs."

"I did hear that!" Bonnie said, laughing. "He was arrested for disturbing the peace and obstructing the movement and flow of traffic."

"I hadn't heard he was arrested. That's funny. Does he really think that picketing would help his court case?"

"When is *your* court date?" Bonnie asked.

"September 25th."

"Good, now that I'm free as a bird, I won't have to take the day off from work that day. I'll pick you up and drive you there if you'd like."

"That would be good. I'll be too frazzled to drive that day. Plus, if they take me out in handcuffs, then at least my car won't be stuck in the courthouse parking lot."

"They aren't going to arrest you. I have to believe in the justice system. You didn't take the money. You were set up. I guess you stepped on someone's toes along the way."

"I'm worried."

"What are you worried about? You didn't steal that money. I knew I didn't like that Officer Williams. Can't trust a guy who looks *that* good. He's just some rookie cop who was told to get you out of the way."

"What do you mean, get me out of the way? Have you heard any buzz? Any idea who might have wanted me out of the way?" I asked her.

"Probably the mayor wanted to create a job for her butt-ugly friend. Won't she be surprised when the charges get dropped and she has to give you your job back?"

"I don't know if I want my job back. How could I face everyone there after they dragged me out of the building in handcuffs and smeared my name all over the newspapers? It's not like anyone would respect me. How could I work for the mayor again if what you say is true— that she wanted me out of there and told them to arrest me? I am so embarrassed. I'm borrowing money from my parents to pay the bills. I might have to sell my house. Uncle Lou would be rolling over in his grave right now if he knew I had to sell the house he entrusted to me."

"Stop worrying. You won't have to sell your house. They will have to give you the back pay when you're proven innocent. You could also sue them for wrongful arrest. Did you know that Tex is going to testify at your trial on your behalf as well?"

"No, I didn't know that. I haven't talked to him since I was arrested. I didn't want to put him in an awkward position by calling him. He hasn't called me either."

"He may not have called you, but he is keeping tabs on you."

"I'm still worried."

"Hey, if all else fails, I'll tell everyone I witnessed Officer Williams whip out his junk and ask you to suck it. Then when you said 'no,' he charged you with stealing money."

"That would be perjury."

"It was just an idea."

"Thanks anyway."

"At least you got a quick court date and this will be over soon."

"I think my lawyer pulled some strings. Have you heard anything more about the safety paper?"

"No, nothing, but you said the State was on furlough until today."

"Is it me, or do you think it's convenient that I'm gone and now you're gone, so that no one is there that would have details about the safety paper?"

"What are you saying? You think there's a connection?"

"I'm not sure. It's a random thought I had."

"That's a pretty serious allegation. Did you tell anyone that?"

"Who would believe me and not chastise me if I were wrong? I don't want to get myself into any more trouble than I am already in. I think I'm going to let sleeping dogs lie on this one. I have a baby to worry about and what people did or didn't do at the municipal building doesn't matter much to me any longer. My only hope is that I can find a reasonable job somewhere, without all this drama, and move on with my life. I'd be perfectly fine if I never had to set foot in Sunshine again."

"But you love Sunshine."

"Used to."

"Your parents still live there. I still live there."

"Which means I don't have a choice but to go there from time to time, but I still don't like it. I have a bad taste in my mouth."

"Bitter."

"And you're not?"

Bonnie took my hand from across the table. "You're just stressed about all this. I promise you, everything is going to work out—for *both* of us. It always does."

"Thanks for being a good friend," I told her.

# 13

Four and a half weeks had gone by without much news about Sunshine. I was busy spending lots of time with my daughter. She was crawling, babbling, and eating baby food now. She always put a big smile on my face and she certainly took my mind off my impending case. Whenever I thought about the possibility that I could serve jail time for a crime I did not commit and be torn away from my sweet baby girl, I would become so overwhelmed with emotions that I would sob uncontrollably. I know Mr. Schubert said that jail time was not likely, but from time to time, my mind would picture the worst-case scenario.

Over the past several days, I had been working with my attorney on my defense. He did his best to convince me that I would win the case. It was finally September 25th. It was a beautiful Indian summer type of day without a cloud in the sky. The vacation crowds were mostly gone. It was the type of day where you wanted to take off and relax on the beach with a good book. But not today; it was my court date.

I had given myself Montezuma's Revenge from my anxiety about today's case. Bonnie was on her way to pick me up. I hoped I'd be able to stay out of the bathroom long enough to get to the courthouse and then long enough to get through the trial. My parents had taken Mandy overnight. They thought it would help me to get some rest, but I wasn't able to catch any sleep. My case was being heard at ten a.m. I was meeting my attorney at nine to go over any last-minute details.

I heard a knock at the door. Bonnie walked in, looked me up and down, and said, "You look green."

"I don't feel so well," I said.

She sat me down on the couch, went to my cupboard, and took out some meds. She poured me a glass of water, handed me a couple of pills and told me I'd feel better in a little bit.

The case couldn't be heard in Sunshine's Municipal Court, as it was considered a conflict of interest. We had to go to a court outside of the county in a town I wasn't familiar with. Bonnie plugged the address into her GPS. I couldn't even pay attention to where we were going, there were so many worries running through my head.

We arrived at the courthouse at eight thirty and we were greeted by my parents at the main entrance. My dad was holding Mandy. My mom immediately gave me a huge hug. I saw my attorney parking his car. My hands wouldn't stop shaking. My dad hugged me and I kissed Mandy on the cheek.

We pushed through the main doors to the courthouse. The courtroom was immediately in front of us and there was a hallway leading to the left with several wooden benches. Court was already in session. We all walked down the hallway and took a seat to wait for our turn.

Bonnie and I went over our testimonies with my attorney. Mr. Schubert felt we were as prepared as we were going to be. I had the jitters and was trying my hardest not to show my emotions. I told myself to be strong over and over again. It felt like the longest wait of my life, then they finally called my name.

We all entered the courtroom. The room was much larger and much nicer than Sunshine's courtroom. It was set up movie-theatre style with cushioned green fabric seating. The dais was finished in a dark cherry wood and there were tables in front of the dais to the right and to the left of the judge's chair.

My parents took a seat in the back with Mandy, I assumed so they could make a quick exit if she acted up. Bonnie had a seat in the first row. Mr. Shubert motioned for me to take a seat at the table on the left side. He sat next to me. My nerves had gotten the better of me and I could barely remember the court proceedings. I recall the bailiff announcing, "All rise. Judge Caton presiding."

I couldn't recite exactly what was said during the trial, but Bonnie and Tex testified on my behalf saying that I routinely took large bills to the bank for change. There was a sworn statement from the former municipal clerk read into the record about how making change for the daily cash drawer was a regular duty for the employees of the clerk's office.

Officer Williams and Mayor O'Donnell had been called to testify for the prosecution. I couldn't look at them while they were on the stand. I had a different feeling toward them now and it was the opposite of admiration. I felt they were both very harsh in their words toward me. I truly believed the mayor was out to get me after hearing some of what came out of her mouth. I remember thinking how two-faced she was. Nice to me in person, then plotting behind my back to get me out of her way.

When both sides rested, Judge Caton ruled from his bench. "Not guilty."

I blew out a sigh of relief, cupped my hands over my face, and started to cry. I could hear my family, Bonnie, and Tex cheering. I found it almost hard to believe—justice had prevailed. I wanted to run over to my parents and Mandy and hug them all, but I had to wait until the Judge finished talking. He said, "The prosecution has not met its burden of proving that Ms. Alton was guilty as charged. Ms. Alton you are free to go."

I turned and gave my attorney a big hug. "Thank you, thank you!" I whispered to him. I ran over to my mom and dad. I hugged them both together, with Mandy in the middle of us. I took my daughter from my dad's arm and kissed her little chubby cheeks.

I saw Mayor O'Donnell pass by me. We all watched as she blew out of the room in a huff. I couldn't help but give her a dirty look. Tex and Bonnie came up to us. My parents hugged them both. I couldn't stop thanking them. If it weren't for them, I wouldn't be off the hook.

My attorney negotiated with the town council for my return to work on October 1st, along with full payment for the time I was on leave. I was dreading returning to work. There was a part of me that felt disgusted by the mayor for doing this to me and I didn't want to see her ever again. There was another part of me that was eager to get back to work to show her that she didn't break me.

• • •

There was a chill in the air and it was drizzling. The weather prediction was for rain the entire day. Mandy woke me at five thirty in the morning. I liked that she was starting to sleep a little later. I fed her breakfast and put her into her Pack 'N Play while I showered. I took extra long in the shower, letting the warm water run down my body. I guess I was procrastinating since I wasn't looking forward to going back to that hellhole I called work. I decided I would suck it up and go back because I had to. I needed the money, but I was only going to stay until I found another job.

I had brushed up my résumé last week and started to keep an eye out for leads. Municipal clerks' jobs are few and far between. It's not customary for clerks to switch jobs quickly. I would basically have to wait for someone to retire or die.

Bonnie thought I should sue the town for wrongful arrest. I wasn't sure about that. I didn't have tenure yet. If I sued Sunshine, I was sure to be out of a job in shortly over a year when my three-year appointment expired. Although, if Mayor O'Donnell won next month's election, I might be out of a job, anyway, since she would probably lobby the council members to get rid of me. At the end of my appointment, they could just let me go for no reason. Bonnie believed the mayor would win the election and I'd be out on my derrière so I should sue anyway. Her argument is compelling because the mayor had been in office for almost twenty years now, so there was no reason to believe she wouldn't be voted in again. I also wasn't sure if suing the town would be frowned upon by other municipalities where I might be seeking a job. Would they be understanding or would they not hire me, fearing I'd sue them too? I was sure that if I sued, prospective employers would Google my name and see newspaper articles about the case. I supposed I should wait for November's election to be over before I made a decision.

I dropped off Mandy at my parents' house and drove over to the municipal building. I sat in the car for a few minutes, not wanting to go inside. I slid out of my car and opened my umbrella. I reminded myself to keep my chin up. The first employee I encountered was Lorraine Paso. She had frizzy, over-processed hair and to say she was obese would be kind. I had heard from Tex that they had amended her title from "Acting Clerk" to "Aide to the Mayor" since I was returning to work. I found it funny that they let Bonnie go, claiming budget cuts, but found money for a mayor's aide. Bonnie definitely had a case if she sued.

"You must be Lorraine," I said with a forced grin. I extended my hand to shake hers as I sized her up. I took an instant dislike to her. Probably she was a friend of the mayor, who was not on my list of favorite people. I knew I shouldn't play that game—the one where friends of my enemies become my enemies, but I was very bitter and not quite over what had happened to me yet.

"Chelsey, I presume. Let's make a deal now. You stay out of my way and I'll stay out of yours."

Rude! I changed my mind. I didn't dislike Lorraine because of Mayor O'Donnell. I didn't like her because she was offensive.

"Fine by me, Lorraine. Let me just get to the point. I have been out of the office for quite some time. I need to be brought up to speed. How is the election coming along?"

"I really haven't done anything with elections. Bonnie was handling all of that."

"So, in the past month when Bonnie wasn't here, none of the election work has gotten done?"

"That's what I said."

*What a bitch,* I thought. I turned and went into my office without uttering another word. I was sure that there was a lot more that didn't get done in the past month other than elections. I got to work right away on the piles and piles of papers sitting on my desk. I don't know why I expected an employee with no experience to have completed some of this work before my return. I can't imagine what Mayor O'Donnell was thinking when she hired this woman with no experience, then fired the only person left who knew how to handle the multitude of tasks this office did on a daily basis.

Throughout the day, I noticed Lorraine was loud and obnoxious to all our residents. She *was* ugly, just like Bonnie said, but not because she wasn't very attractive; it was because of her rude personality. If she had been a regular hire for my office, I would have taken the time to train her on customer service. Since she would run back and tell the mayor anything I said or did, I opted to keep my distance.

Late in the day, I came across the salary resolution for Lorraine, which was approved at a previous council meeting. I almost soiled my pants. They were paying her over

$120,000.00. Who the heck gets paid that kind of money and doesn't know the job, doesn't do any work, and is rude to customers? I didn't think it was possible to feel more nauseated by Mayor O'Donnell or Sunshine, but I did. I made a copy of the resolution and stuffed it in my purse.

At four thirty, I closed up shop and dialed my mother to let her know I'd be a little late today. I had to make a stop. I drove over to Bonnie's house. She was in the middle of making dinner.

"Hey! This is a nice surprise!" Bonnie said. "I'm cooking lasagna; do you want to stay for a bite?"

"I'd love to, but I have to go pick up Mandy. I only have a few minutes," I told her. I reached into my purse and pulled out the salary resolution. "Maybe this is all the proof you need that they didn't have budget issues when they abolished your position." I handed her the paper.

Bonnie took a few moments to read it. Her eyes got real wide. "I should be mad that they are paying her so much money when they were paying me next to nothing, but this just made my day! Wait until my attorney gets a load of this!"

I smiled. "Wild, isn't it? I mean, the mayor claims there is no money for a guard to make people go through metal detectors daily, no money for an alarm system, no money for any safety precautions, but she found plenty of money to create a job for her buddy."

"And now they are going to have to find plenty of money to pay me when I sue their pants off!"

"I gotta go; I'll see you soon," I said as I walked down her driveway back to my car.

"Thanks, Chelsey!"

# 14

*I* felt frustrated from the moment I woke up. I decided to stop at Take Ten after I dropped off Mandy and treat myself to a cup of coffee. When I pushed through the door to the shop, who did I see? Lorraine having coffee with none other than Mayor O'Donnell. They suddenly stopped talking when I walked in, as if they were saying something they didn't want me to hear. The sight of them made me sick. I ignored them and asked the barista for a large crème brûlée-flavored coffee. I wished they had shots of something to make my coffee stronger to get me through the day.

While I was waiting for my drink to be prepared, Officer Williams entered the coffee shop and sat with the mayor and Lorraine. If I had realized that Take Ten was going to be a big hangout for the Sunshine Brown-nosing Club, I would have skipped the cup of joe and gone directly to my office.

I drove to work. I took a deep breath and counted to ten before getting out of the car. Inside, I stared at the mounds of work draped over my inbox. I was basically expected to do everything myself, since Mrs. Ugly sat on her behind all day not doing anything. I looked down at my phone. Thirteen voicemails were already waiting for me. I guess word got out that I was back at work.

I listened to a few messages from coworkers who said they were happy to have me back. That made me feel a little better. At least some people appreciated me. The fourth message was from a woman named Mrs. Coral who had been trying unsuccessfully for three weeks to get someone to call her back with instructions on how to get a copy of her husband's death certificate. No surprise there—that Lorraine wasn't answering phones and wasn't calling people back. I hit the callback button to dial her number. She didn't answer the phone, but I left her a message to stop in today and see me if she could or to call me back.

I finished listening to my messages. It was ten o'clock by the time I returned all the calls. Mrs. Coral was at the window five minutes later. I apologized to her for the wait and explained I was out on leave for a while, having only returned yesterday. I handed her a form to fill out and took a copy of her ID.

The computer networks were running slow today. I asked Mrs. Coral to take a seat while I waited for an internet connection in order to check to see if the death had been properly recorded. She wanted five certified copies. I unlocked the drawer where we stored our Vital Statistics paper. I panicked for a moment. There was no paper. Then I remembered that Bonnie moved it to a new hiding location after we had discovered the paper was missing.

I grabbed the key to the liquor license cabinet and retrieved the paper from there. The pack of paper seemed rather light to me. I was immediately suspicious of Lorraine. She would have been the only other person who knew where the paper was kept and it didn't sound like she had been bothering to issue any certificates to the public, so I was curious to see exactly what was missing.

I finished waiting on Mrs. Coral. She was very appreciative that I had helped her. Then I put on my invisible detective hat and got down to investigating. I pulled out the logs of destroyed safety paper and noted how many pages were purposely shredded. I pulled out the receipt books from the past month and a half and counted the number of copies issued for birth, death, and any other life events. I confirmed the sequential numbers of the safety paper that had been previously missing with notes I had made when I originally realized paper was missing. I double-checked bank account figures with our CFO to see how much money had been deposited from the sale of certified records. My suspicions were realized. More safety paper was missing.

I waited for Lorraine to go to the bathroom, then I called Bonnie.

"Hey, Bonnie, I have a quick question for you. Does anyone know where you moved the safety paper to?"

"It's in the liquor license cabinet."

"I know that, I'm wondering who else knows."

"Just Lorraine, why?"

"There is paper missing again, at least a hundred sheets."

"You've got to be joking. Maybe you should call the county prosecutor or something. Or those FBI guys that interviewed you. Something's wrong and if I'm thinking what you are thinking, then that witch mayor and her ugly friend need to be behind bars."

"My thoughts exactly."

I hadn't noticed Lorraine had returned from the ladies' room. I hoped she didn't hear anything. I quickly switched the subject.

"Do you want to get together for lunch this weekend? It's Columbus Day weekend, so I have off on Monday," I asked Bonnie.

"I know you are changing the subject on purpose; someone must be listening."

"Yuppers."

"Is it ugly?"

"Hell, yeah."

"Monday is good. Hey, maybe we can check out that Bratz place again. Maybe your knight in shining armor will be working since it's a week day."

"Monday it is then. I'll pick you up around eleven thirty."

"See you then, Chelsey."

"I'll see you, Bonnie."

I didn't want to risk Lorraine hearing me on the phone again, so I emailed the state registrar. I told him I was concerned that this was the second time this year that I had noticed the safety paper missing in my office and I implored him to put a ban on the issuance of certified records from my office until such matter could be investigated.

Seconds later, I received a reply. Invalid email address. I know I hadn't typed the address wrong, I chose it from my address book. I went to the State's website. It said that Beverly Daniels was the interim Registrar of Vital

Statistics. I wondered what happened to Mr. Alfred. I decided to do a Google search for his name.

What I found next was troubling, to say the least. Charles Alfred had been murdered near his home about a month ago. I couldn't believe I hadn't heard anything about this. The news article said it was a mugging gone wrong. I felt queasy at first, then I felt frightened. Could it be possible that this had something to do with the fact that I had contacted him about the missing safety paper here?

I knew I shouldn't surmise without having any facts. I went over the particulars in my head, making a mental list in no particular order:

1. The safety paper is missing.
2. The FBI raided Town Hall looking for mayor's records and vital statistics records.
3. I alerted the state registrar to the missing paper.
4. The state registrar is dead.
5. I knew about the paper.
6. I was accused of a crime I did not commit.
7. Bonnie knew about the paper.
8. Bonnie was fired for a bogus reason.
9. Lorraine was the only person who knew where the safety paper was moved to, other than Bonnie.
10. More paper went missing.
11. Lorraine is Mayor O'Donnell's friend who got a job making more money than any other employee in Sunshine.
12. The mayor could be placed at the scene of the crime within twenty-four hours of the burglary, flood, and computer/phone tampering incidents.

13. There was also an arson, making that four attempts to sabotage the building with no arrests made.

That was more than a dozen facts. I was starting to connect the dots. Was I being paranoid or had my suspicions all along been accurate? I truly believed the mayor was guilty. I wasn't sure about Lorraine. Either she was involved or she had some real good dirt on Mayor O'Donnell and was blackmailing her for a job.

I used my lunch break to call Agent Romeo and spill my guts about all of my suspicions, but I only got his voice mail. I was feeling apprehensive. If I was right and they killed Mr. Alfred, then what would they do to me? They already had me arrested. They knew where I lived, what hours I worked, the names and address of my parents. Would they hurt Mandy to get to me? I shuddered at my thoughts and hoped that I was overreacting. I had accused Bonnie of being a drama queen, but maybe that title suited me more.

After lunch, I tried to drown myself in work to get these insane thoughts out of my head. If I kept busy, I wouldn't feel so afraid. I had to keep telling myself that I concocted the notion of the mayor being an arch criminal and that I was making it all up to exact revenge on her for having me arrested. After all, I was absolutely, without a doubt, a disgruntled employee.

Later that day, I received a call back from Agent Romeo. I excused myself to go sit in my car to talk to him without Big Brother's prying ears. I recited my list of facts to him and told him to take it for what it was worth. I didn't want to be held accountable if something bad happened and I never informed some kind of authority.

"Must be nice to be able to leave the office whenever you want," Lorraine squealed at me as I walked back in the room.

There were so many things I wanted to say—it must be nice to make $120,000.00 per year and not have to lift a finger to do anything, for one. More than saying something, I wanted to shove my boot into her mouth and knock a couple of her teeth out. But, instead of sarcasm and violence, I opted to kill her with kindness. I just smiled and went back to work.

• • •

There was a terrible stench filling the lobby when I entered the building for work on Wednesday. I noticed public works was painting the hallways and stairwell. I went to my office and opened up the windows. Even though it was nippy outside, I was feeling lightheaded and needed the fresh air. Exhaustion, frustration, and anxiety had taken its toll on me this week. I reminded myself that I already made it through two days back at work and if I could make it through the pains of labor, I could make it through the rest of this week. I contemplated seeing a doctor and getting some happy pills to make work seem more bearable.

Lorraine came in to work late again today. "Did you oversleep?" I asked her sarcastically.

She squawked back at me with her nose in the air, "No, I had a meeting with Mayor O'Donnell." I guessed that was her new excuse for showing up whenever she felt the urge.

"Mayor O'Donnell wants this office to be used as the official mayor's office since there isn't one in the building. She wants you to move into the basement. She already made arrangements and had public works move a desk down there for you," Lorraine announced.

"Is that so?" I asked.

*Oh, so the bad little girl that I am is getting banished to the basement,* I thought. *Unbelievable.* The mayor was rarely ever in the building; there was really no need for a mayor's office and if she thought there was, then *she* should have been put in the basement. I marched out of my office and over to Rodney's to see if I really had to move into the basement, where there were no other offices. I tried to point out to him that the senior citizens that came in to pay their taxes and get their beach badges or dog licenses at the same time were not going to want to trudge downstairs.

"It wasn't my decision," Rodney said without even looking up at me.

I walked back into the hallway and went to the ladies' room to cool off. After thinking about it for a bit, I realized I'd be just fine and dandy getting away from Lorraine in my face all day every day, so moving to the basement wasn't such a bad idea.

Upon entering my office, I promptly announced that I was happy to move and I'd be doing so immediately. I grabbed a cart, disconnected all my computer wires, and loaded up my computer, printer, and all of the paperwork I was currently working on. I dialed the number to the public works department and asked them if they would be able to move my phone as soon as possible and to move the rest of my file cabinets when they had time.

I purposely packed the safety paper and the cash box. I wasn't taking any chances. I decided to mix the safety paper in with a bunch of files so that it couldn't be readily seen by Lorraine on my way out. When my cart was filled, I headed out to the elevator. It appeared the stairwell was off limits to residents today too, because of the painting going on. It finally made sense why the mayor was having the stairwell painted, I guess she wanted it to look somewhat presentable to the people who have to come in to my office. After all, these were the same people that would be voting in November when her current term was up.

The elevator was taking forever today. I didn't understand why. There was only this floor and the basement in the building. The doors started to open slowly and I heard a horrible screeching sound. I hesitated for a minute because I thought it sounded bad.

"Hiya, dolly," I heard from behind me. I turned around to look and saw it was Rose Sciaratta. I gave her a big smile. I liked Rose.

"Rose! How nice to see you. What brings you here today?"

"I came to see you."

"You did? What can I do for you?"

"I want to know if I can pick up the poll books and supplies for my district. I get paid an extra twenty-five dollars for that, you know. An old lady like me is on a fixed income; I could use the extra money."

"Sure, Rose, no one else has called me yet, so I'll put you down. I'll have everything the day before the election, just come in…"

I was interrupted by an ear-piercing squeal. Rose and I both stuck our fingers in our ears.

"That don't sound good, honey," Rose said.

"I know," I said as we took a step back from the elevator.

The elevator rumbled, then crashed to the ground. The entire building shook. The crash was so loud, I thought a bomb had detonated. Dust flew up from the shaft and permeated the air. We covered our faces. I grabbed Rose's arm and escorted her out of the building as fast as her arthritic old legs could go. Policemen were running across the parking lot from headquarters and entering the municipal building. Sirens from the fire trucks were blaring in the distance. Employees were running out of the building, coughing.

It wasn't until I was safely in the parking lot that I realized if Rose hadn't stopped me, I might have been inside the elevator when it plummeted to the basement level. I felt choked up and I gave Rose a big hug.

"Rose, I think you just saved my life," I told her.

"Now, now, sweetie, you're okay. We're both okay," she said, patting me on the back.

There usually wasn't anyone in the basement, but Rodney was outside taking a head count just in case. When he was sure all of the employees had made it out, he told us all to go home for the day. On my way to pick up Mandy, my paranoia set in. Several questions floated in my head:

*Was the elevator tampered with? Was the accident meant for me? Was the mayor trying to have me killed?*

# 15

It was Columbus Day and I was thrilled to have a four-day work week. I was due to meet Bonnie for lunch. I lived a little closer to Jackson than Bonnie did, but since I had to drop off Mandy, I told Bonnie I would pick her up.

Bonnie's house was powder blue today. "You had your siding painted again?" I asked her.

"I get bored and now that I'm no longer employed, I have too much free time on my hands."

"Your husband must want to kill you."

"Just a little. I told him I did it for him since he hated the pink. He keeps telling me to find another job."

"I'll drive today since you drove last time."

"Works for me! That means I can have a couple of drinks."

We hopped into my car and I turned out of her driveway toward the causeway. Driving in my Honda Accord was quite a large step down from Bonnie's fancy Mercedes. Bonnie turned and looked behind her.

"That's strange," she said.

"What's strange?" I asked.

"That black sedan behind us. It had been sitting across the street from my house for the past hour and now it's following us. All the windows are tinted."

"You're starting to be paranoid like me," I told her. "It's not surprising they are following us; this is basically the only route off the island."

"I suppose."

We continued driving off the island and through Madisen Township. I opted to take the back roads to Jackson to avoid traffic.

"Speaking of being paranoid, I have a story to tell you about the elevator at work..." I started to say when I was interrupted by the sound of a car revving its engine and speeding up behind us. I glanced into my rearview mirror and could no longer see the bumper of the black sedan. Then *smack*! We were jolted forward upon the impact. The black car hit us. I slammed on the brakes and the sedan swerved to my left into the lane of oncoming traffic.

"What the hell?" Bonnie screamed as we felt a second impact in the side rear panel of the driver's side. My car was pushed over into the right shoulder. I held tight to the steering wheel, trying to force it left. It was all I could do to keep the car on the road. The black car slammed on its brakes and shot behind us when a tractor-trailer was approaching it head-on. It then revved its engine again, coming for us from behind.

Bonnie yelled, "Speed up! They're going to hit us again."

I frantically pressed the pedal down like she said. I could barely think. I tried to reach over to my purse and grab my cell phone, when *whack*! We were hit again, thrusting us forward. My head hit the steering wheel. My purse and its contents went flying. I was afraid the airbags would go off and I wouldn't be able to see. My heart was pounding. I was terrified.

"They're trying to kill us," I said in a panic to Bonnie.

"Well, they're not going to be successful. See if you can get them to pull up alongside of you again."

"What? Are you out of your freaking mind?" I shouted. "You want me to get next to them? They probably have guns!"

"Well, so do I," Bonnie said as she reached into her purse and pulled out a small handgun.

"Where the heck did you get a gun?" I asked.

The sedan pulled into the left lane again and increased in speed in an attempt to get alongside of us. I crouched as low as I could behind the steering wheel, took a deep breath, held it, and tried my best to hold the car steady. My whole body was trembling.

Bonnie rolled down her window and climbed halfway out, aiming and shooting at the black car. "*Pop, pop, pop.*" She fired three times. I heard car tires screeching and I looked into my rearview mirror to see that the mystery car had veered off the road and was smoking. I started to breathe again.

"Good shot," I said as I sped off down the road as fast as my demolished Honda would go, trying to get away as quickly as possible.

"Thanks. My husband and I go to the shooting range on occasion. It's a hobby of ours. We went this Saturday. I had forgotten to take the gun out of my purse. Good thing!"

My heart was in my throat. My hands were shaking uncontrollably and I was still in a frenzy. I had gone into survival mode and now that the adrenaline was wearing off. I think I was going into shock. "Are they following us? Where do you think the nearest police station is? Are you going to get in trouble for shooting a gun? Would you call 9-1-1 from your cell phone?"

"I'm already dialing. I don't think they are following us, but keep driving just in case. Make a bunch of turns so they don't know where we went. And no, I don't think I'll get in trouble for shooting a gun. I have a permit, and it was self-defense. *And*, if I do get in trouble, it's better than being dead. Plus, I have enough money for a good attorney."

I found an old diner and parked behind it, where my car couldn't be seen. I wasn't sure where we were. Bonnie gave our location to the police, then the two of us went inside and sat in the back, near the kitchen, so we could make a discreet exit out of the service entrance if we so needed.

We both ordered coffee. I had lost my appetite. "Too bad we didn't find a bar instead of a diner. I could use a stiff martini right now," Bonnie said.

"I could use a whole lot more than one martini," I said. "A bottle of them would be nice."

"Did you get a license plate on that car, by chance?"

"Heck no, I was too busy trying to stay on the road. I guess you didn't either?"

Bonnie shook her head.

"Do you know what the make or model was?" I asked her.

"Not a clue. I know what you are thinking; you are thinking Mayor O'Donnell put a hit out on us," Bonnie said half jokingly.

"What other scenario makes sense?"

"Who knew where you would be today?"

"Only my parents, unless one of our phone lines are tapped. Do you have any enemies you aren't telling me about?" I asked Bonnie.

"Lorraine hates me and the mayor fired me."

"Lorraine!"

"What?"

"Lorraine may have overheard my conversation with you earlier in the week. *She* would have known I was meeting you for lunch today."

"Maybe you're not off your rocker after all. You better call those FBI guys and let them know."

"I will."

The local police arrived and took a report. They said I shouldn't be driving my car, so they had it towed for me. The damage was extensive. Bonnie called her husband to give us a ride home.

"So much for Bratz," Bonnie said.

"That's the least of my worries," I said as I pulled out my phone. I called Agent Romeo and gave him the scoop on what happened. Jayce dropped me off at my parents' house and I had to explain to them why I didn't have a car.

"That's it!" my father exclaimed. "You are not going back to that evil place you call work. There are more important things than that hellhole. You go home and get your things, and you are staying with us. You have a daughter to worry about now and you are not safe living there alone."

I felt like a five-year-old child being scolded. I knew he was right. I wasn't safe and this wasn't worth me taking my life into my hands. I could probably go out on stress leave; I certainly had enough stress! I borrowed their car and drove back to my place to gather what I needed for a long while.

Packing for an eight-month-old was not a quick and easy task. It was good that my parents babysat Mandy, because the big items were at their house already, like a swing, highchair, and crib. As I was running around the house throwing necessitates into a bag, the phone rang.

"Hello? Hello?"

No one was there. I shrugged it off and kept going. I had a lot of things to gather. I took out a suitcase and started packing up my clothes. A few moments later, I heard a noise outside. I froze. I could hear my heart beating. I was terrified it was the people from the black car coming to kill me again. I reached under my bed for the baseball bat I kept there for emergencies. If someone was there, I wasn't going down without a fight. I turned off the bedroom light and stayed there, hidden in the dark. I saw a shadow of a person outside the bedroom window and heard the doorbell ring.

I ran to the phone in the hallway, dialed 9-1-1, and told them someone was trying to get in. I heard the window in my bedroom shatter. Without thinking, I ran toward the window with my bat and swung as hard as I could at the hand that was trying to lift open the window. I made contact. There was a yelp from a man's voice. I screamed out, "I called the police five minutes ago; you'd better get running." I could hear sirens in the distance, which made me feel reassured that I would be safe.

An extremely nice female police officer from Madisen Township named Patricia took my statement, while others collected evidence. She stayed with me while I packed my things. The premises were searched, but no traces of the perpetrators were found. I asked Patricia if she could call Agent Romeo and tell him about the incident. When I told her about the situation that occurred earlier in the day, she provided me with a police escort back to my parents' house.

My parents were alarmed to see the police vehicle with me. Patricia waited until I was settled inside. Mom cried when I told her someone tried to break-in. Dad took out his old hunting rifles and bullets. He wasn't taking any chances.

• • •

Against my parents' wishes, I went in to work the next morning. I wanted to clear out the personal items that I had in and on my desk, like my photos of Mandy. My plan was to find a psychologist to write me out of work on stress leave. If the mayor wanted me gone, I would be gone, but I was going to make darn sure that I was still getting paid.

I pulled out the personnel manual to refresh my memory on the policy for disability leaves of absence. Lorraine strolled into the office an hour late. She looked surprised to see me. "Oh, you're here," she said. "Why wouldn't I be?" I retorted. She stuck her nose in the air and turned to walk out of my office. "Make sure your time sheet reflects that you were late again today," I said to her. I figured I had nothing left to lose and that I wasn't coming back to work anyway.

I finished reading the personnel policy manual when I heard someone ask for me at the window. It was a sheriff's officer delivering another lawsuit. I signed for the document and chuckled to myself when I saw Bonnie's name written as the plaintiff. Bonnie was suing for wrongful termination.

I scanned the court papers and was about to email them to Mr. Betts when Tex arrived in my office. He closed the door behind him.

"Your father called me and told me what was going on," he said.

"Then you also know that this is going to be my last day of work for a while."

"Don't go out on leave just yet. Wait until after tomorrow."

"Why would I want to do that?"

"Trust me; it will be worth your while. There is a staff meeting scheduled for tomorrow morning. You won't want to miss it."

"If you say so," I said, leery of what he was saying.

# 16

The day the FBI agents raided Town Hall for a second time was a day I wouldn't soon forget. The date that was to be engraved in my mind was 10/10. All the department heads were in the morning staff meeting with the mayor, when we saw multiple vehicles descending upon the municipal complex. We all rushed to the windows to see what was going on.

Somewhere in the neighborhood of twenty agents stormed into the building and blocked off each entrance. We all filed out into the hallway and toward the lobby to get a better look. It was surreal. The agents were dressed in black pants and ties. They each wore a blue windbreaker with FBI imprinted in bright yellow on the front and back. They were brandishing badges, weapons, and handcuffs. They rushed over to where we were standing and approached Mayor O'Donnell, who spoke up and said, "I demand to know the meaning of this!"

"Mayor O'Donnell?" one of the agents asked. She nodded. "You are under arrest. You have the right to remain silent, anything you say can and will be used against you…"

She interrupted them. "I know my rights. I want my lawyer!" she yelled as they cuffed her and dragged her out.

Another agent turned to me and asked, "Lorraine Paso?"

I pointed to Lorraine, who was standing in the doorway to the clerk's office.

It was a pleasure watching them handcuff her, drag her out of the building, and shove her into the back of a vehicle.

A third agent handed me a subpoena for records. I pointed them in the direction of my office and said, "You are welcome to whatever you'd like." Shortly thereafter, Tex came in and pulled me aside.

"I suppose you know what's going on," I said to him.

"Yes. I kept telling you to trust me."

"Did you know this was going to happen when I was in jail and you told me to trust you?"

"Yeah, I knew this was going down. I have been working with the FBI for over a year now. I just couldn't tell you any details."

"So, what *is* going on?"

"Well, the mayor was behind the missing safety paper in your office."

"I suspected as much," I told him.

"She was trafficking personal identifying information. When they initially raided Town Hall, they already knew that someone on the inside had been involved in issuing fake vital records. They planted bugs around the building in hopes they would get a lead. You led them to O'Donnell with your suspicions."

"So I guess Lorraine was involved, since she was just arrested?" I asked.

"Yes."

"I wasn't sure if she was involved or if she just knew the dirt."

"She was the go-between for the people buying certificates. The buyers never knew the mayor was involved."

"Who was buying the records?"

"A variety of people. Illegal aliens. Teenagers wanting to buy alcohol. People involved with identity theft. People collecting insurance money from deaths. There are lots of reasons people purchase fake IDs."

"Were they caught?"

"A few of them were. That's how the FBI got involved with the investigation in the first place. They discovered some of the fake documents when someone tried to apply for a passport with one. They alerted the Motor Vehicle Commission to be on the lookout for other suspicious documents issued by Sunshine Township. Lorraine had assumed an alias for use with her clients, so even though clients were being arrested for false documents, it took quite a while to figure out who was involved in the issuance. Initially, they covered their tracks very well."

Tex continued, "Later on, they caught Officer Williams when he faked someone's death and claimed the insurance money. He provided them with a death certificate from your office. He rolled on the mayor in order to get himself freed from the charges. The FBI was looking to fry a bigger fish."

I was absolutely shocked by this news. I knew he was chummy with the mayor, but I would never have taken him for a criminal. Turned out that Bonnie was right when she said she there was something about him that she didn't like. And to think I wanted to date him! Between him and my ex, I am terrible at choosing men. I guess it's the bad guy thing that I'm attracted to. I'd really like to meet a good guy for a change.

"I would have never known he was involved. He seemed like a good guy. Why would he do all this?"

"Looks can be deceiving. He had financial troubles and desperately needed to get his hands on some money."

"Why did Lorraine and Mayor O'Donnell do this?"

"Money? Power? Maybe a combination of both. What typically happens is that people do something criminal for a particular reason, like needing money. Then, when they realize they didn't get caught, they get a God complex and think they can do whatever they want and not ever get caught."

I asked him, "What did that have to do with me? Why did they have me falsely arrested? Did they know I suspected them?"

"Lorraine Paso was blackmailing Mayor O'Donnell. Lorraine wanted a cushy job in the town and was threatening to expose the mayor if she didn't get one. The mayor feared you could be on to her, since you knew about the missing paper. She surmised you would figure it out eventually, so you were a good candidate to remove to make space for Lorraine. Basically, they wanted you out of the way for a while. Plus, they knew if they were charged with a crime, that you wouldn't make a credible witness against them since you had an arrest record for theft yourself."

"Assholes! Oops, sorry, I just couldn't contain myself there for a minute," I said.

"Was it the mayor who tried to have me killed?"

"Officer Williams admitted that after arresting you didn't keep you out of their way, the mayor had decided to get rid of you permanently. He rigged the elevator to crash in exchange for a large payment from Mayor O'Donnell. When that plan didn't work, she apparently hired another couple of goons to take you out."

"Did you find the goons?"

"There are two suspects in custody regarding what happened to you this week, both with the car incident and the attempted break-in at your house. It's only a matter of time before they substantiate Williams' story."

I was thankful that the mayor's plan was foiled and I was still alive. I felt some satisfaction in knowing she would be going to jail for a very, very long time. I felt disgusted that Officer Williams was getting off scot-free, but I knew karma would take care of him in the end. At minimum, he would lose his job.

Tex went on to tell me the rest of the details. Back in March, Officer Williams was the one who had set the courtroom on fire. He had hoped the building would burn to the ground, so that there was no evidence of the safety paper missing. He hadn't counted on anyone noticing the fire until it was too late.

Once Williams told that story, he offered up the rest of the details in exchange for immunity. He and the mayor had orchestrated the robbery at the clerk's office. This was to cast doubt that they had taken the paper, hoping it would appear that an intruder took it. They messed up the HVAC system to try to destroy the paper so it would be assumed the paper had to be discarded instead of missing.

Tex said, "According to Williams, when the mayor knew you were about to contact the state registrar, she tampered with the computer server and cut the phone lines in hopes of postponing your correspondence with him until the goons she hired could get rid of him."

"That's insane," I said. "Did they think the state registrar was the only person who worked in that office and that I would have no one else to contact if they killed him?"

"I guess she was desperate to cover her tracks. The mayor also concocted the bedbug story to try to create a defense for herself."

"How would that be a defense?" I asked. "The paper was already missing when the exterminators came to the building."

"She is going to try to put the idea of reasonable doubt into the minds of the jurors by showing evidence that multiple people were frequently in your office. That multiple people had the access and the ability to take the paper."

"That's a stretch."

"Yeah, I know."

I was sickened by the fact that this whole time, I had blamed Mr. Triggers in my head for all the sabotage around the building. I would have sworn up and down that it was he who had caused the mayhem. He seemed nuts and Mayor O'Donnell and Officer Williams both seemed normal. I felt appalled that I was tricked into thinking the two of them were good people for a while. My first impressions of them both were incredibly wrong. I suppose my impression of Mr. Triggers was off the mark as well. I should have known early on that the mayor was involved by the way she kept asking me about the safety paper. I should learn to trust my instincts more than my brain.

"Why did they make the decision to arrest them today?" I asked Tex.

"Partly because they finally had enough evidence. Partly because they knew your life was in danger. Possibly because the mayor was up for election this year and some politician didn't want her reelected."

"So what kind of punishment will they get?"

"If they are found guilty, jail time and hefty fines for issuing over 50 false records. Attempted murder carries a large sentence."

"I hope the judge throws the book at them. I was certainly fooled by them, I used to think the mayor and Officer Williams were good people, I guess I am a horrible judge of character."

"It's not you, Chelsey, they had us all fooled at one time."

# 17

After a nice long reprieve, Robert Triggers showed up at the window first thing this morning. *Oh, just wonderful*, I thought. I had gotten through a terrible ordeal and made it out alive and I thought it would be easy going from now on. I decided to be nicer to him, even though he was a pest. I had him pegged all wrong and I felt the need to give him the benefit of the doubt. I told myself he was just a resident looking for a solution to his problem and he was passionate about getting something accomplished. He hadn't been in my office in two months. I could certainly be pleasant to him.

"Hey idiot. You said that plans for my road didn't exist," he promptly announced.

"I'm sorry, Mr. Triggers, let me pull out my files; this is going back a while."

I found the records request form asking for the plans, which was submitted by Mr. Triggers back in August. This jogged my memory. I denied the request on the basis that no records existed.

"I have your request here, Mr. Triggers. I recall that I did try to locate the plans, but your street was built so long ago, I did not have any luck."

"Who told you the plans don't exist? You're too stupid to figure that out yourself. Someone is out to get me and I want to know who."

"Mr. Triggers, I can assure you, no one is out to get you. I went to the archives myself and looked for the plans. I could not find any."

He seemed to get angrier than he already was. "I know you people are out to get me. Almost every time I'm here, you won't give me what I want!"

I tried to sound reassuring. After all, I had decided that I was going to be polite to Mr. Triggers today, but I'm sure the words came out of my mouth more condescending than anything. "I am certainly not out to get you, Mr. Triggers. I always give you the documents I have and I give you a reason if I'm not able to give you something. In this case, I also double-checked with the planning and zoning secretary, who told me that she could not find any plans for your street. She does not know who you are and is absolutely not out to get you either."

Disgruntled, he screamed, "Fine! Whatever! But I'm telling you that the mayor is out to get me. She sends the police after me all the time. They have me arrested for no reason. I spend all of my free time here because I want my dunes! No, no, let me rephrase that, I *need* the dunes. My house is not going to be protected in a natural disaster. They are ruining my life!"

"I'm sorry, Mr. Triggers, but I have nothing to do with the dunes or the mayor. I am only the keeper of the records. In addition, the mayor might not even be working here much longer."

"Yeah, I read that in the newspapers. I knew that wench was a dishonest, lying bitch. I hate her."

Hate is such a strong word. I reserve it for a few special people that I've encountered in my life. My ex is one of those people. The mayor is another. I thought to myself, *If Triggers only knew my true feelings for the mayor, maybe he wouldn't view me as the enemy.* However, I was too professional to express my opinion to any member of the public who wasn't in my close circle of friends and family.

"Is there anything else I can help you with, Mr. Triggers?" I asked.

"Yes, as a matter of fact there is!" he said as he handed me a long list of records he wanted.

Mr. Triggers proceeded to look through various records for the next hour, having me fetch different documents on his command. He was trying my patience, but I kept reminding myself to be understanding. He took about fifty pages of copies, then left. I was shocked when he said, "I hope you have a nice day" on his way out. By the tone of his voice, I wasn't sure if that was sincere or if he was giving me some type of strange warning.

I went back to my desk to find a message from Mr. Betts, asking me to call him back. I dialed his phone number. "Hi, Colby. It's Chelsey. I am returning your call."

"Howdy, Chelsey. How are you hanging in?"

"Just fine. Thanks for asking."

"Chelsey, I need you to do a favor for me. I need you to draft a resolution for tonight's agenda for a closed-session discussion about litigation, *Triggers versus the Town of Sunshine.*"

"I had almost forgotten that you were in court for that yesterday. I'll have the resolution ready to pass out tonight."

"Great, that would be just wonderful. Just so you know, we won the lawsuit with Mr. Triggers."

"Oh, that makes sense. He hadn't been in the municipal building since he filed his suit and he came in today for more records."

"He's probably looking to appeal."

"Thanks for letting me know, Colby."

I took a second to breathe and look around when I got off the phone with Colby. Ah, no Lorraine. No Frita O'Donnell. I quietly enjoyed a moment alone, thinking things would go back to normal now. But things weren't normal yet. Bonnie wasn't here. I wished that council would reinstate her since the mayor and Lorraine were arrested, but I doubted that she would be rehired now with her lawsuit pending.

The council meeting for tonight was probably going to be strange without Frita acting as Chair. I predicted there would be complaints from the public about what had happened and that it would be a stressful meeting. I guessed, technically, until Frita was convicted, she didn't have to give up the position of mayor. I found it ironic that when I was accused of a crime, they immediately made me give up my position without pay, and so far, there was no talk about the mayor having to give up her position without pay. I wondered if this also meant that Lorraine didn't have to give up her job either.

I picked up the phone and dialed Tex. He answered the phone, "Detective Texidoro."

"I don't know if you'll have the answer, but do you know if Lorraine or Frita are getting out on bail?"

"It's doubtful. The judge set bail pretty high. Last I heard, neither of them made bail yet."

"Well, if they are able to make bail, do you think they will be coming back to work?"

"I could see Frita maintaining her innocence until the bitter end."

"Do you know when they will go to court?"

"I haven't heard anything about a court date. It could take up to six months."

"Did you say six months?" I asked. I didn't like that answer.

"Yes, six months or more. I really don't know."

"Do you think I should get a restraining order?"

"You certainly could if you want to."

"I'm asking your opinion."

"I will call you the second I hear anything about either one of them making bail."

"Thanks."

I hung up with Tex and marched over to Rodney's office. I opened his door and said, "I'm here to make sure that there is fair treatment of all employees."

He looked at me, confused.

"I'm talking about the mayor and Lorraine. Since you put me on 'administrative leave' without pay when I was arrested—falsely, I might add—then you should be putting those two out on leave without pay as well."

"Not a problem with Lorraine. Frita is a different story. I don't have the power to do that. There are laws."

I went back to my office and dialed Mr. Schubert. A woman's voice answered the phone, "Law office."

"Is Mr. Schubert in?" I asked.

"No, I'm sorry; he's in court all day. May I take a message?"

I left a message telling him I wanted a restraining order against Lorraine Paso and Frita O'Donnell and I needed to know how to do it. One or both of them tried to have me killed and I wasn't taking any chances on making Mandy an orphan. I wasn't waiting for one of them to post bail.

• • •

I received a call from Bonnie early Monday morning. She knew she could call me after five thirty because I was up feeding Mandy.

"Hey," she said.

"Hey! What are you doing up so early? And what are you doing, calling me? You usually text me and tell me to call you," I said with a giggle.

"I just had to tell you my news."

"Oh?"

"I am dropping my lawsuit in exchange for my job back with a raise, back pay, my attorney's fees, and a settlement for my pain and suffering."

"Are you serious? The mayor agreed to that?"

"No. According to Colby, council can take a vote at their next meeting on the terms of my settlement. They don't need the mayor's vote to make a majority, and the other council members will approve it."

"Do you think they will go for it?"

"Oh, I think they know they don't have a snowball's chance in hell of winning my suit, so they either take it or the town loses a heck of a lot more than what I'm asking for and gets some bad press."

"Wow! That was really fast. We just got served less than a week ago."

"The powers that be didn't want any more negative publicity for the town, given what just went down with the mayor. My timing was impeccable."

"Well, then let me be the first to say, welcome back!"

"You missed working with me."

"I did. And Mr. Triggers missed you too."

"Ugh. I forgot about him. Is he back bothering you? Maybe I shouldn't come back to work."

"Why *are* you coming back? And yes, he *is* back."

"My husband's after me to get back to work."

"Is he finally tired of you changing the siding on your house?"

"You don't know the half of it."

"I don't think I want to know!"

I was relieved that Bonnie was coming back to work. I needed her, not only to help with the workload, but to help keep my sanity. I made it through Thursday's council meeting fine. Triggers wasn't there, Frita wasn't there, and there was no drama for a change. I wasn't sure I'd be so lucky at the next council meeting, which was in less than two weeks. I couldn't wait to have Bonnie back.

I hung up with Bonnie, put Mandy in her crib, and got into the shower to get ready for work. I heard my phone ringing, but decided whomever it was could wait. I was going to be late to work if I didn't get moving. I got dressed, quickly dried my hair, and slapped on makeup. I put Mandy and her diaper bag in the car, then drove to my parents' house. After dropping her off, I looked at my phone to find a missed call from Tex. I dialed him back.

"Hello, beautiful," he said.

"Uh oh," I replied.

"What 'uh oh'?"

"You're about to tell me something I don't want to hear. You always try to ease the blow with a compliment when you are about to dish out bad news."

"You know me too well."

"So, what is it?"

"Mayor O'Donnell was bonded out."

"When?"

"A couple of hours ago."

"Ugh."

"Sorry to be the bearer of the news."

"Thanks for letting me know."

I was happy that I went forward and filed for an emergency temporary restraining order on Saturday with the Madisen Police Department. I wished that the county court offices had been open so that I could have filed for a more permanent order, but Mr. Schubert hadn't gotten back to me until Friday night and the court was closed over the weekend. I planned on calling the county court later today to figure out what I had to do.

I made copies of my temporary order and distributed it to everyone who needed to make sure I didn't have to be near the mayor. Rodney, Colby, the eight members of council, the police department. I wanted everyone to know that she was required to stay away from me.

I found myself biting my nails and not getting much work done. I couldn't work like this. I hoped that those who were not fans of Frita O'Donnell would step up to the plate and call for her resignation. I hoped she lost the upcoming election.

I picked up the phone and dialed Bonnie back.

"Hi. Sorry to bother you again."

"You're no bother," she said. "Shouldn't you be at work by now? What's up?"

"I am at work, but I just learned that Frita is out of jail. I'm so worried, I can't think straight. Do you think you can take me to buy a gun and teach me how to shoot it?"

"I don't think she'll try to go after you again. It would cast a tremendous amount of suspicion on her if you were to end up dead."

"I don't care; I need to protect myself and Mandy. I want a gun."

"Okay."

"Can we go now?"

"Now? You're going to leave work?"

"Yes, this is important, I'll tell them I have an emergency and I'll take personal time."

"Okay. Come on over."

I left an email for council telling them I had to leave unexpectedly, then I drove to Bonnie's house to pick her up. We drove over the bridge to go to the police station in Madisen. I asked the police records clerk for the form that I needed to fill out to purchase a handgun. She handed me the form for the permit and a clipboard. I took a seat and carefully filled in each section. I returned it to the clerk when I was finished and she asked me to take a seat.

After ten minutes, Patricia appeared in the lobby and said, "So, you are getting yourself a gun."

"Hi, Patricia," I said. I was a little embarrassed. I didn't think I'd run into anyone I knew and I felt silly being so scared that I wanted a gun.

"Come on back," she said as she directed me to a small room where she took my fingerprints. Patricia informed me that it could take as long as six weeks for the fingerprint checks to come back.

I paid the fees and thanked Patricia for her help. Bonnie and I exited the building and jumped back in the car.

"Six weeks is a lot longer than I expected. What am I supposed to do to protect myself in the meantime?" I asked Bonnie.

"I have some pepper spray at home. I'll give it to you. I would also recommend a good alarm system."

"Good idea."

Next, we drove to the sporting goods store a few miles away from the police station in Madisen. We walked up to the gun counter and started looking.

"May I help you?" said the old man behind the counter.

"Just looking," I said.

He directed us to where the pocket-sized guns were located. I never realized there were so many varieties of handguns and I felt overwhelmed.

"What kind of gun do you have?" I asked Bonnie.

"One of my guns is a Ruger LC9," she said as she pointed it out.

"One of? How many guns do you have?"

"I don't know, five or six."

I should have known better. Bonnie had more than one of everything she owned. When you have money, I guess you can buy multiple "toys."

I read the description of it on the tag in front of the display model. It said it was a double-action-only, hammer-fired, locked-breech pistol with a smooth trigger pull. This might as well have been written in Arabic. I had no idea what it meant.

"I don't know what I'm looking at," I told Bonnie. "This is beyond my comprehension."

"Maybe I should have just taken you to the shooting range and let you try my guns first, then see if you like any of them. I don't have time this morning, but let's schedule a day to go."

I dropped Bonnie off and thanked her. She told me to let her know what day worked for me to go to the range. She also told me she would go with me to buy my gun when my permit came in.

I drove home and called an alarm company. They were willing to come out right away to install the alarm. It took them the remainder of the afternoon to install all the motion detectors, hardwire everything, and give me instructions on its use. I felt safer already. I bought the model that talked. It would say things like, "The back door is open." I thought this was a great feature since Mandy would be walking soon. I would instantly know if she tried to open any of the doors.

I went back to my parents' house and picked up Mandy. I thought it best not to tell my parents what I had learned about Frita being released or what I was up to all day. They were already scared sick about my safety. I didn't need to give them something else to worry about.

I decided to stop at the grocery store on the way home. I loaded Mandy into the cart and went into the store. I needed to buy some baby food and I didn't have any food for myself in the house. I was in the cereal aisle when I saw Mr. Triggers coming toward me. *Oh crap, not now*, went through my mind.

"I need to talk to you," Mr. Triggers said to me. Again, he smelled to high heaven. My eyes started to tear. What was that smell? Onions? Mandy started to cry. She was at an age where she didn't like strangers and she probably got a whiff of his bad body odor too. I decided to pretend I was someone else.

"I'm sorry, do I know you?" I asked.

He looked confused. "I'm Robert Triggers," he said.

"Have we met before?" I asked.

"What are you talking about?" he said. "You know darn well who I am."

"I don't think we've met before. Are you one of my customers at the dry cleaners?" I imagined this man had never set foot in the dry cleaners by the way he smelled, so I felt I was safe making up that occupation.

"Dry cleaners?" he asked. "Are you on drugs? You know me from the municipal building."

"Oh! You must be talking about my twin sister Chelsey. I'm Christine. We look exactly alike."

"Oh," he said and he turned and walked away with a baffled look on his face.

I chuckled to myself. I thought it was pretty clever of me to think of that. I wasn't in the mood to deal with him outside of work. He would have taken up all my time and I needed to get done and get home.

# 18

The next morning, Mr. Triggers was at my office bright and early.

"I met your sister yesterday," he said.

"We don't get along," I said. "How may I help you?"

"I need to look through those boxes again."

I had totally forgotten about the boxes. I don't know why he was saying "again." He hadn't bothered to come in and look through them the first time! It was irritating knowing that he was going to make me go through all the trouble of getting those boxes a second time, then probably never come back to look at them, just like before.

"Do you know which boxes you needed?" I asked.

"All of them!" he demanded.

I made him fill out a records request form and told him I'd have them by noon tomorrow. Shockingly, he left without an argument.

Bad memories of the boxes came flooding back to me as I picked up the phone to request them from storage. I felt embarrassed all over again when I remembered tripping over them in front of a bunch of men from the public works department. I also suddenly remembered all those fire alarms we were having back then and realized I hadn't heard an alarm since I had been back. I guessed they finally fixed the problem. I laughed to myself at Bonnie's firemen comments, or "Bonnie-isms," as I recently started calling her candid remarks. I missed Bonnie and couldn't wait for her to come back to work.

• • •

Boxes upon boxes arrived in the municipal building the next day. I grew disgusted just looking at them. I put in a work order for public works to bring me a table and chair for Mr. Triggers. To my surprise, Mr. Triggers showed up at two o'clock to go through them. I told him he was welcome to have a seat and help himself to the boxes.

By four o'clock, he hadn't made a dent in searching through the boxes. He approached my window and told me he had to leave, but he would be back the next day. The next day, he arrived at eight thirty in the morning. He asked me if he could come inside and use our computers.

"I'm sorry, Mr. Triggers, we do not allow residents to use our computers for safety reasons."

"What safety reasons?" he said.

"To prevent acts of sabotage," I responded.

"What kind of sabotage?"

"The kind that ruins computer networks."

"I'm not going to ruin any computer networks. I just want to set up a spreadsheet to record the documents I'm looking at in these boxes."

"You're welcome to bring your own computer in to use, but I cannot allow you to use our computers."

"Why not?"

Irritated, I said, "I just explained that to you."

"Explain it again."

"It's not our policy to allow residents to use our computers."

"I want to see that policy," he said, growing agitated.

"It's not a written policy."

"Then I'm allowed to use them."

"No, you're not."

"Then I want to speak to someone who knows what they are doing around here," he screamed.

Rodney was out for the day, so I didn't know who to get for help. I wasn't going to be speaking to the mayor. The council members were all at their full-time jobs. Triggers was not going to take no for an answer and with him being so adamant and my patience running out, I decided to call the police to diffuse the situation.

"I'll be right back," I said.

"Where are you going? I'm not done talking! I will not be ignored!" he yelled.

"I'm not ignoring you; I'm going to get someone else in here, like you asked."

I hurried into my office and dialed 9-1-1. I was so frazzled, I wasn't even sure what I said to the dispatcher who answered the phone. Within seconds, Detective Texidoro arrived with another officer and our town's K-9. Mr. Triggers didn't seem to notice the dog.

After ten or so minutes of Mr. Triggers trying to convince Tex that he should be allotted appropriate time to utilize the town's computers, Tex grew weary and told Triggers he had to leave. When Triggers refused, Tex said that Triggers was creating a disturbance with his shouting and he would be escorted out of the building if he wouldn't leave peacefully. As Triggers' voice increased in volume, the dog became progressively more agitated.

With both hands, Triggers shoved Tex. The other officer let go of the dog and the dog attacked, biting Triggers in the arm and not letting go. Triggers kicked, squealed, screeched, and screamed in agony. He fell to the ground with the dog still latched onto him. The dog growled and flung his head from side to side tearing open the skin on Triggers' arm.

"Call it off! Call it off!" he shouted.

The officer called off his dog. I tried my best not to laugh. I mean, the man was hurt. Blood was trickling down his arm out of the puncture wounds. But it served him right for putting his hands on an officer. Tex then arrested him for assault. This maniac was racking up quite the rap sheet. Assault by egg, assault by coins, assault on a police officer, assault with a picket sign. Well, I don't think the picketing arrest was an assault, but it *was* another arrest. I thought he was a loose cannon and I wondered what types of antics he would try next.

Triggers was processed and bonded out within a few hours. I was rattled when I saw him in the parking lot on my way out of the door for the evening. He started to follow me to my car. I reached into my purse and clutched the pepper spray Bonnie had given me. If the pepper spray didn't work, my plan was to grab his bandaged arm, then kick him in the nuts and run like hell.

I turned around and said, "Why are you following me? What do you want?"

"I want to know why you called the police." He looked at me with a sinister glare.

"Don't you see how you act? You intimidate people. You berate people. You are condescending, insulting, mean and aggressive. You scare people."

I hurried to my car, jumped in, and turned over the engine. I looked back and Triggers was getting into his own car. I blew out a sigh of relief. I drove to my parents' house and picked up Mandy. On my way home, I saw Triggers' car in my rearview mirror.

"You freak," I said out loud to myself. "You better not be following me."

I told myself not to panic. Maybe it was just a coincidence. Triggers lived on Fourth Street. Maybe he had stopped at the grocery store and was merely driving home. I kept my eye on him. When we passed Fourth Street, my red flags went up. I drove over the causeway with Triggers hot on my trail. I made a couple of unusual turns to make certain he was following me. He was. I reached into my pocketbook and dialed the Madisen Township Police Department. I told them that an infuriated resident from my work was following me and I feared his intent was to do harm to me or my infant child. I told them I was afraid to go home and I would meet them at a local shopping center.

A Madisen Township police car was sitting near the entrance to the shopping center when I got there. Triggers saw the police car and drove off. I pointed the car out to the officer and gave them Mr. Triggers' name. He took a report and said I could come down to the station to file a complaint. I needed to get Mandy home to feed and bathe her, so I opted to forgo the complaint and report the lunatic to Tex later tonight.

Installing the alarm system in my home was proving to be the right thing to do for my peace of mind. I wished I was also able to get that gun by now, but I still had weeks to wait for the permit. I found myself jumping out of my skin at every little sound. After seeing the K-9 today, I thought about getting myself a dog too. A Doberman or a Pit Bull. Something with big teeth. The alarm helped to calm my nerves, but it wasn't enough to make me feel secure. I was on full alert.

Once I put Mandy down to sleep, I called Tex on his cell phone.

"I was followed by Triggers tonight," I said.

"What do you mean, 'followed'?" Tex asked.

"I left work, picked up Mandy, then noticed him following me in his car on my way home."

"Did you call the police?"

"Yes, I called Madisen Township's police; they met me at a shopping center. Triggers took off when he saw me pull up to the police car."

"Okay, so did you file a complaint?"

"Not yet."

"Why the hell not?"

"They said I had to come down to the station. I had to get Mandy home, I'll do it tomorrow."

"So, why are you calling me?"

"So nice of you to be concerned."

"I am concerned, but you need to get it on record and file that complaint."

"Why do you think he was following me?"

"Who the hell knows what goes on in that deranged brain of his."

"Do you think he was going to hurt me?"

"Look, if it makes you feel better, I'll run his name through the system to see if he has any major priors. I'll call you right back."

Nail biting was fast becoming a new bad habit of mine. I was anxiously awaiting a call back from Tex. Fifteen minutes later, I got the call.

"You're not going to like what I found."

"I don't care. I need to know what I'm up against."

"Oh calm down, I found nothing."

"Nothing?"

"Nothing that you didn't already know about. The egging, the pennies, the picketing. All things aimed toward getting his dunes back, I guess. I don't think you have to be worried. I don't see any violent acts."

"What about how he pushed you?"

"I was in his face; he did step over the line. Do I think he would do that again? Not really."

"Not to you he wouldn't, and not in front of a dog," I said.

"You could probably get a restraining order."

"The courts are going to think I'm the crazy one, taking out another restraining order on a different person trying to kill me."

"How do you know he was trying to kill you?"

"I don't. So, if he wasn't trying to kill me, how would I get a restraining order granted?"

"For stalking."

193

"I don't know, he's already on the edge. I feel like if I do anything to push him over it, then he'll do something to hurt me. I'm not ready to do a restraining order yet. I have enough people trying to do me bodily harm."

"Well, keep it in mind."

Talking to Tex didn't help ease my mind or help me to gain any shuteye, but I'd be worse off if he had told me that Triggers was a serial killer.

• • •

The next morning, I was more cautious and vigilant than usual. I carefully checked all around the house for any suspicious cars or strangers lurking around. Because of the mayor and Triggers, I trusted no one. I kept my pepper spray in my hand, just in case.

I made it to my parents' house and to work without any problems. I thought to myself, *I cannot continue to live like this*. I knew I needed to find a different job, hit the lottery, or something. I opened up the newspaper when I got to work and I saw that the mayor's court date was scheduled for April. April seemed like a lifetime away. I would surely have ulcers by April. Even then, there was no guarantee that Frita would go to jail and no guarantee she wouldn't try to exact revenge on me.

My thoughts were broken by a voice saying, "Hello?" I stepped out of my office and saw a Sheriff's officer waiting patiently at the window for my signature. I took the envelope from him and signed his paperwork. I tore open the package. It was an appeal filed by Mr. Triggers. If he didn't win the first suit, I didn't know how he would win the appeal. I faxed it over to Colby.

I recalled that Triggers stopped coming by my office when he first filed suit. I hoped that he would do the same this time. I glanced down at my ringing phone. The caller ID showed it was Mr. Triggers. The man must have ESP. I felt uneasy and quickly chose not to answer it. He left a voicemail saying, "Chelsey, I didn't mean to scare you yesterday; I just wanted a chance to apologize. I didn't mean to be disruptive or make you upset. My actions were intolerable and I hope you will accept my apologies."

"That was unexpected," I said out loud. I debated whether I should still go down to Madisen Township during my lunch break like I had planned. After contemplating it all morning, I decided to leave well enough alone. If Triggers tried anything again, I would go right away to file a complaint. Tex said he wasn't violent and I didn't want to cause him to become out of control by filing a complaint against him. I also didn't feel like going to court to face him about a stalking complaint.

# 19

The weatherman announced a post-tropical cyclone would be hitting our region this week. I wasn't quite sure what a post-tropical cyclone was, but it sounded dreadful. We had been through tornados and nor'easters, but never a cyclone. News reports were predicting tropical storm force winds, hurricane-like conditions, and potential tornados. It sounded worse than a hurricane, yet they dubbed it "Hurricane Sandy." I also heard it being called "Frankenstorm," which seemed more appropriate.

Our disaster preparedness team was ready to take action. I was part of the team. I was in charge of managing the emergency phones and ensuring the opening of the Sunshine's shelter in the senior center. In the aftermath of a storm, I was also the one in charge of coordinating donations.

Our police department opened a twenty-four-hour Emergency Command Center. I prepared our standard press releases, indicating school and activity closures and evacuation routes. Flooding was a serious concern in our town. We are surrounded by water. A storm surge would certainly do some major damage.

Within twenty-four hours, Sandy turned from her path of grazing the coastline and was headed for a direct hit to the island. Sunshine was in terrible danger.

I immediately issued a press release to evacuate the island. I had our IT consultant post the release on our website, Facebook page, and through a blast email. Unfortunately, residents didn't take us very seriously at first. The weather seemed way too nice for a storm to be approaching. It was literally the calm before the storm.

I prepared notices to cancel tomorrow's council meeting. Normally, this would be the decision of the mayor, but since I wasn't talking to her, I went forward with the cancellation. I told Rodney to tell her the news. He was acting as an intermediary between the two of us. I felt fortunate that Mayor O'Donnell kept her distance and had left me alone thus far.

I was relieved about the meeting being cancelled. I hadn't yet worked out how I was supposed to be at the meeting with the mayor running it. I didn't know why she refused to step down. I was going to work it out with Bonnie so that she would be the one covering the evening council meetings for the remainder of the year. I was hoping Bonnie would be willing to do this because Bonnie didn't seem as afraid of the mayor as I was. Since Bonnie knew her way around a gun, I wouldn't be surprised if she would plan on showing up at the meetings packing. After this year, I was hoping the mayor didn't win the election so that I wouldn't need to worry about not being able to work the meetings. Then, in a few more months, the mayor would have her trial and be put away. Now with the storm and the meeting being cancelled, Bonnie couldn't officially be reappointed as planned.

At lunchtime, I was able to leave work and fill sandbags for myself. Although I never experienced the lagoon flooding, I wasn't taking any chances. I did my best to load my bags into the trunk of my car, then I headed back to work. I was working overtime tonight and probably the next night.

By the time the five o'clock news came on, people knew this was no joke. Residents started calling our hotline in a panic. I tried to keep the callers as calm as possible. I gave out instructions on how the evacuation would be handled and where sandbags could be filled. I reminded them to take their medicines with them. There were several residents who had no family and nowhere to go. For those callers, information about our shelter was given, which would be open at eight o'clock the next morning. The rain was supposed to start at that time.

The police sent out a reverse 9-1-1 call, instructing all residents that the evacuation was mandatory and they had until three p.m. the following day to leave. At three thirty, the causeway coming into the island was to be shut down.

I worked until eight o'clock that night since we had plenty of volunteers to take over the phone lines. I knew my parents had already packed my dad's SUV and their plan was to leave by six a.m. They were taking Mandy for me and heading to my cousins' house in Lawrenceville. I headed home to cyclone-proof my house. I had to be at work the next day, and might even have to operate the shelter during the storm, but I wanted to be prepared in case I was told to evacuate as well.

I carefully placed all the sandbags around my backsliders. I gathered up my medications, some clothes, a blanket, a pillow, my important documents, and toiletries and threw them into a carry-on-sized suitcase. The only things of value that I owned consisted of a diamond pendant given to me by my grandmother and my former engagement ring that I planned to hock one day. I threw them both in my pocket.

I moved everything that I could to higher ground. The top of my entertainment center was filled with knick-knacks. I used the top shelves in my kitchen and closets for as many items I could fit. The top of my refrigerator worked as a nice shelf as well.

It was already midnight and I was wiped out, but I still had Mandy's things to go through. I threw boxes of diapers into the car and I packed a duffle bag full of her clothes, rash cream, towels, and a few toys. I loaded the bags of her baby food, bottles, and formula in the car also. Two hours later, when my car could barely fit me in it, I locked up and went to bed.

• • •

At five o'clock in the morning, I woke up and couldn't fall back to sleep. My internal clock must have reset itself since I was waking up with the baby every morning. I showered and dressed in jeans, a T-shirt, and sneakers and headed out to work early. The rain hadn't started, but gloomy dark clouds covered the sky.

My first stop was at the municipal building. I made sure that anything of importance was moved out of the basement. We didn't need our computer server and other equipment ruined if the basement flooded. I then moved everything possible off the floors and out of the lower drawers of the filing cabinets. I did the best I could to protect the records and small pieces of equipment from flood waters.

When I arrived at the Emergency Command Center, I was alerted to a change of plans. There would be no shelter on the island. The cyclone was producing gale-force winds with gusts as strong as eighty mph. There would be major power outages. The surge would be crippling, if not devastating. The decision was made to turn off the gas to the island by six o'clock in the evening, before the storm was anticipated to make landfall, in an effort to prevent fires.

I manned the phones, which were ringing off the hook, while volunteers went door-to-door making sure that everyone knew there was a mandatory evacuation. Flyers were passed out with a checklist of what people should pack. Reflecting back on this past year, on all the things that I thought were terrible, I realized that none of it mattered. Everything I had gone through with the identity theft ring seemed to pale in comparison to this. This storm was going to affect every single person in Sunshine. I was worried that everyone, including me, would be safe and left unscathed from the storm.

It was four o'clock and time for the emergency workers to make their way off the island. I squeezed into my car and headed toward the evacuation route. Traffic had been bumper-to-bumper all day, but it was moving now, albeit slowly. I anticipated arriving at my cousin's house no later than six since the pace was sluggish, the rain was at a steady pour, and the wind was gusting powerfully at this point. It was dark and hard to see so I was appreciative of the fact that I could take my time driving.

Once I eased onto the highway, car speeds picked up to forty mph. My mind started to wander. I was troubled by the thought of my house being destroyed. I hoped that everyone left Sunshine and was sitting in a cozy living room with relatives that were far away from the deluge.

I pulled up to James' and Daisy's house and breathed a sigh of relief. I made it and I could see that my parents made it. I parked at the curb and let myself in their front gate. They lived in a large old colonial. Their home had four bedrooms, if you didn't count the basement and attic apartments. My parents were staying in the basement, which was equipped with its own kitchen, bathroom, shower, living room, and dining room. Mandy and I were sleeping in the attic, mainly because it was too many steps upward for my parents' feeble knees to handle.

I stepped up to the front porch and rang the doorbell. James greeted me at the door. I said hello, then headed right over to where my sweetie pie was playing with her blocks and gave her a big hug.

"Mommy missed Mandy," I said.

I heard my mother behind me. "Oh, thank the lord you are here. I was worried sick about you! I wished you could have left with us. I was bothered by the fact that you may have had to stay there in Sunshine with this storm."

James and my father unloaded my car while Daisy and I hoofed everything upstairs. When we were done unpacking, Daisy fixed me a plate of leftovers. I don't think I remembered to eat all day and the smell of the chicken and mashed potatoes warming in the microwave sent hunger pangs to my belly. After I finished eating, I joined everyone in the living room. It was after seven by now and Mandy was sound asleep on the floor. I picked her up and brought her upstairs where I had set up her Pack 'N Play and put her to bed. I changed into my nightclothes and crashed as well.

At midnight, I was awakened by the sound of the cable box clicking off. *Power just went out,* I thought. A beat later, it clicked back on. "Full-house generator. Good investment," I said as I rubbed my weary eyes.

I found the remote and clicked on the TV. On every channel was news coverage of the storm. They announced flooding, heavy rain, and strong winds. Sandy made landfall at eight o'clock that night. High tide was around ten o'clock. The storm surge was peaking now. It wasn't until they showed the preliminary video footage that I started to cry. It was still dark out, but you could still see enough to tell that practically everything on the east coast was under water.

I left the bedroom to go downstairs to my parents. I stood near their bed in the basement, clutching the baby monitor in one hand and placing my other hand on my father's shoulder. He roused.

"Dad," I whispered in a still shaky voice. "It's all gone. Our homes are gone."

He jumped out of the bed, flew to the TV, and pressed the power button. The reporter said, "This is the worst storm in the history of New Jersey; the devastation is unparalleled. We have never seen anything like it."

My father and mother looked at each other and broke down in tears. I had never seen my father cry before. I was heartbroken. We all continued to watch the news while we hugged each other and wept. The damage we saw was unspeakable. Some areas looked like houses were placed in the middle of a riverbed. Entire homes had washed away. Millions were without power in Maryland, Delaware, New York, and New Jersey.

By two o'clock in the morning, I knew I had to get some sleep. Mandy would be up in a mere three hours and I couldn't stand by and do nothing. I knew I needed to go help Sunshine tomorrow somehow. I closed my swollen eyes and tossed and turned until it was time to get Mandy's bottle ready.

• • •

The sun was rising. The storm had passed, but left a trail of ruin in its wake. By seven o'clock, I was showered, dressed in sweats, and ready to go.

"Are you out of your mind?" my father growled at me without taking his eyes off the television. "You can't get over the bridge; it's still flooded. What on Earth do you think you are going to do to help out?"

"I don't know, Dad, but I'm on the Emergency Management Team and I need to find out what is going on and where I'm needed. I have an election to worry about too. I'm responsible to run that election, no matter what."

"For heaven sakes, Tom, go with her and help her. Maybe you can see how bad the house is," my mother said.

I heard him grumble something under his breath. I was sure he was cursing us both. None of us had gotten much sleep the night before and I didn't think he was prepared to see what had happened to his neighborhood.

We jumped in the car and were on our way. Traffic was minimal. The Governor had declared a State of Emergency, which was still in effect.

"What on Earth are you going to say if we get pulled over? We're not supposed to be on the road," my father said.

"All I have to do is show my work ID, Dad, and they will understand that I need to be there to assist in any way possible."

It took us nearly two hours to get to Madisen. We were detoured several times by downed trees and power lines. Many traffic signals were down due to the power outages. At first, we saw mainly broken windows and missing roof shingles. We seldom saw another car on the road. As we continued to drive east, we saw homes in shambles. One home was literally sliced in half by a grand old oak that had uprooted. I prayed no one was hurt, but it seemed unlikely for my prayers to be answered.

Since I made it to Madisen, I made the decision to check on my house before anything else. There was a pole down, so I parked a block away, and we walked to my house. I kept my fingers crossed as we approached the driveway. I could see that the gutter had pulled away from the roof. The storm shutters were still in place. The siding was splashed with mud. I had a sinking feeling in the pit of my stomach as we opened the front door. Electric was out. I peered around the living room, which looked okay. We moved to the kitchen, where I saw a puddle of water on the floor where the roof leaked. The food in the refrigerator had spoiled and the ice from the freezer had melted, causing another puddle.

I checked out back. My fence was gone. Kayak—gone. It appeared the water from the lagoon had risen high enough to cause some problems, but luckily, did not intrude into the house. I breathed a sigh of relief, knowing my home was still here.

"You better find yourself a roofer pretty quickly to fix those shingles or you'll have more water in the house. All the roofers in the area are sure to be booked up with this mess," my dad said, trying to be helpful.

I had been making phone calls the whole drive down to the shore area, but no one was answering. I couldn't figure out what was going on in Sunshine.

"What do you want to do, Dad? I can't get a hold of anyone. Should we try to go over to your house?"

"Well, we drove all the way here; might as well."

I cleaned up the water on the kitchen floor, then locked the front door. We walked back to the car then headed toward the causeway. As we got closer to the bridge on the bay side, the devastation was apparent. Most of the homes along the bay front were obliterated. I noticed military vehicles blocking all lanes, not letting anyone through. I pulled up alongside of a soldier in camouflage fatigues and rolled down my window.

"May I help you, ma'am?" he asked.

"I'm the Municipal Clerk for the Town of Sunshine and a member of their Emergency Management Team. Am I allowed to cross?"

"No, ma'am, I'm sorry. The island is flooded. There is no way to pass in your vehicle."

"Do you know where I can find any of the officials for the town?"

"I'm sorry, ma'am. My orders are to stay here and not allow anyone through. I don't have any information for you."

"Are there any residents stranded in their homes?"

"There are over one hundred National Guard soldiers that were deployed here. If anyone is trapped, we are working diligently to save them."

I thanked the soldier for his time and for serving our county. I looked over at my dad. His head was facing out of the passenger side window and I could still see a tear rolling down his cheek. I knew what he was thinking. His home was probably in shambles. I felt a lump in my throat, but I wouldn't allow myself to cry. I needed to be strong for my dad.

"Looks like I'm out of a job," I said jokingly, trying to lighten things up a bit.

"I suppose so," my dad said.

I turned the car around and headed back to Lawrenceville. I wanted to give my daughter a hug. Even though sadness surrounded us, I was thankful my family was safe.

# 20

*I*n the aftermath of the storm, the only thing we could do was sit and wait. I decided to stay at my cousins' house with my parents since there was still no electricity at my place. I wanted to be near family anyway, away from the horrifying scenes down the Jersey shore. I kept busy making phone calls to various county elections officials, making arrangements for early voting and relocating the polls. I asked our IT department to disseminate information on how Sunshine residents could get their ballots in. Voting may not have been the top priority for some people given the circumstances, but for those who wanted to vote, I wanted to make it as convenient as possible.

Finally, after three days of waiting, I received a call telling me to report to work in the morning. I was left with specific instructions—to bring my government ID, to park my car bayside in a specific parking area, to dress down, and bring work gloves if I had them.

I made the trip to the shore in an hour and fifteen minutes. I parked in the designated area and walked over to a military 4x4. I informed the soldier at the wheel that I worked for Sunshine and I was instructed to park here. After he checked my employee ID and driver's license, he said he would drive me to the rendezvous point, whatever that meant.

As he drove over the bridge, I can only describe what I saw as catastrophic. I grew teary-eyed looking at the ruins surrounding us. I suddenly understood the need for the escort. Without the 4x4, the roads were impassable. Mounds of sand, three feet high in some spots, were dumped into the streets, partly covering any vehicles that were left behind in the evacuation. Houses were either completely demolished or had windows, siding, and garage doors blown out. My driver had to navigate around boats that had been lifted from their docks and slammed down into the streets. Piles of debris were strewn in every direction I looked. Power lines were downed, trees were uprooted, and dunes were gone. The island no longer looked like the island. This was a place I no longer recognized.

As we approached Sixth Street, the damage seemed less extensive. It was clear that the houses had been submerged, yet many remained intact. We turned onto Beach Boulevard and I spotted what was left of Bonnie's house. Her entire first floor was missing. Her upper floors were supported by pilings and nothing else.

I knew that the first floors of beach houses were designed to break away during a major storm surge, but I had never seen it happen before. I felt terrible for Bonnie. I wondered how I would break this news to her. Since residents hadn't been allowed in the island yet, I didn't think she knew about the condition of her house.

We made our way over a couple more blocks to the municipal building, which turned out to be the rendezvous point. I noticed that the building did not seem to have substantial damage on the exterior, except for shattered windows. I hopped out of the military vehicle and went inside, going straight to the clerk's office. I was immediately thankful that I didn't have to worry about disaster recovery for the town's records, especially the historical and permanent documents that were not stored at a second location. Everything was intact and dry. It would have been terrible to lose Sunshine's documented history. I had received a grant to microfilm meeting minutes when I began working for the town, so those would have been safe. Old maps and books would not have been.

The basement wasn't in as good shape as my office. It had indeed flooded and the flood waters remained trapped inside. Without electricity, the sump pump must have not been able to do its job. I headed back outside.

There were people gathered outside, waiting for directives. I joined the crowd. Rodney arrived and gave a pep talk before he handed out assignments. Unfortunately, the dreadful news of twelve deaths in Sunshine was reported to us. I felt sick to my stomach. They were not people I knew, but it was still tragic.

The Army Corps of Engineers was taking part in the recovery mission and providing support to public works. With the knowledge of the fortunate being saved and the less fortunate victims having been accounted for, the next task was making the roads passable. Arriving on site were dump trucks, backhoes, and other pieces of large equipment.

My assignments included phone support, handling resident inquiries, and coordinating non-monetary donations. I was given a cell phone. The main number for the municipal building was to be transferred to this cell phone later in the day. I didn't have to stay on the island; I could work from virtually anywhere. Considering there was no electric or gas, I didn't have a choice but to work elsewhere.

I took a walk over to Thirteenth Street. At first glance, it wasn't that bad. The dunes seem to have protected their street somewhat. I used my key to let myself into my parents' house. Upon closer inspection, it appeared that the first floor had to be completely gutted. I started snapping photos with my cell phone. I figured the insurance company might request them.

The carpeting and drywall were soaked. I assumed the insulation had to be replaced. The appliances in the kitchen were rendered unusable. Furniture could not be salvaged. I made my way upstairs. The second floor seemed to be untouched. I didn't see any leaks through the ceiling, so it appeared that the roof held up.

I locked the front door and exited the house through the back. Their fence was knocked over, but didn't seem damaged to me. The grill was beyond hope of salvaging. The chiminea was metal and starting to rust already. I wasn't sure if the lawn furniture was missing or if my dad had put it somewhere.

The power would be out for an undetermined amount of time so I knew I'd have to break the news to my parents that they would have to infringe on my cousins for a while longer. I was sure they were going to be much more upset about the condition of their house than about having to stay with my cousins. I decided to take more photos of the ruins around the island. Maybe if my parents saw how bad some people had it, they would feel more thankful that it didn't end up being worse for them.

I walked back to the municipal building and hopped on the next military escort, to be taken back to my car. There wasn't much I could do without electricity. On our way back, I noticed the sign for Fourth Street. Fourth Street was unrecognizable. Mr. Triggers had been right all along; without dunes at the end of his street, not one of the houses remained standing.

I drove back to Madisen. I thought I'd check on my house and see if the electricity had been turned on yet so that I could work from there. No luck. I dialed Bonnie's phone number.

"Hi," I said. "Did you survive the storm?"

"Hey. Where are you? I'm at my mother-in-law's house in Rumson. We are all safe. I tried to get on the island to check out my house, but they wouldn't let us in."

"I'm at my house right now, but I have no electricity. I went to the island today. I'm going to work from home for a while, until I can't take the cold any longer. I'm staying at my cousin's place in Lawrenceville."

"You were on the island? Did you happen to drive by my house?"

"Are you sitting down?"

"Chelsey, just tell me. I can take it."

"I didn't want to tell you this over the phone. I am so incredibly sorry, Bonnie. The bottom half of your house broke away during the storm."

Bonnie wept. It was overwhelming. I was numb the whole ride into and out of Sunshine. I told Bonnie that twelve residents perished in the storm. We both stayed on the phone and cried.

"Do you want me to come to your house and help you?" Bonnie asked.

"Not yet," I said. "I don't have much to do at this point. They gave me a cell phone, which will temporarily be the main phone line for the Sunshine. I might need help taking calls tomorrow."

"Was the whole island destroyed?" Bonnie asked.

"Pretty much," I told her.

We hung up, and I found myself a couple of notebooks and pens. I loaded them into a bag with paperclips, a stapler, and some tape. I was going to wait around longer to answer the Township cell phone, but the phone hadn't started ringing yet, so I got in my car and left.

I dreaded the drive back to Lawrenceville that evening. I knew I had to face my parents. I wasn't sure how I would break the news that their house was a mess. I carefully reviewed my speech in my head.

Everyone was waiting for me when I arrived at my cousins' house.

"Well?" my mother asked.

I explained how I had to park off to the left of the causeway and that the military had to drive me onto the island. I told them about how the storm dumped numerous feet of sand onto the roads. I described how Bonnie's house and some homes and businesses were swept away by the ocean. I knew this wasn't what they wanted to hear. My parents were sitting on the edge of their chairs in anticipation that I would tell them about their house next.

"It wasn't that bad in comparison to everything else. The house is there and it is intact. You did get some water in the house. You'll probably have to replace the carpeting, some furniture, and appliances. The upstairs was untouched. The siding needs to be power washed. All of your windows were intact. You may need to replace the drywall and insulation downstairs. You fared better than most others on the island. There were twelve deaths in the storm."

My mother cupped her hands over her face and left the room. I could hear her bawling in the bathroom. My father was speechless.

"I took pictures for the insurance company. I'll show you tomorrow," I told my father.

It was getting late and I didn't want to upset him any more than he already was. I took Mandy and got her dinner ready. Her little face made me smile. She was a little shining light in the midst of all the darkness I had seen today.

# 21

The next day was Halloween, which obviously was cancelled for the children of Sunshine. I felt like I was playing the part of the Grim Reaper when the cell phone started ringing at six o'clock in the morning and it was up to me to deliver the ghastly news. I grabbed my notebook and answered the phone.

"When are we allowed onto the island to get into our homes?"

"There's no set date yet, sir," I replied.

"This is ridiculous. I demand to know why I can't go to my house. It's been almost a week."

I tried to be as understanding as I could. If only this caller could see what I had seen, he would understand. I took his name and number and told him I'd call him with updates.

The next twenty calls were the same. Homeowners and business owners. Men and women. Seniors and college students. All looking for answers. I longed to do more than be the complaint division. It was the next call that made me think harder. The caller asked what she could do to help.

I pulled out my iPad and looked up Madisen Township's website. I found their phone number and called their Township Clerk, Kathy Norcia.

"Hi, Kathy, it's Chelsey Alton from the Town of Sunshine. Do you have power in your municipal building?"

"Yes, we got power back today," she informed me.

"I hate to infringe on you, but Sunshine was reduced to rubble in the storm. We have nowhere to work. I happen to live in Madisen and I was hoping you had a conference room I could use to set up shop."

"Oh, of course. I could set you up in our all-purpose room."

I thanked her and told her I was on my way. I called Bonnie next. "Do you feel like coming to help me today?"

"Sure. Where do you want to meet?"

"Madisen's Town Hall. Are you sure you're okay with this, being that you aren't officially rehired yet?"

"What else do I have to do today? Sit around and mope about my house? I'll be there in an hour or so."

We disconnected and by nine o'clock, I was headed out on the road to Madisen.

The municipal building for Madisen was far bigger than ours. There were large columns in the front with a large staircase. I pushed open the heavy glass double-doors at the main entrance and walked down a long corridor to the municipal clerk's office. The window to their clerk's office was encased in glass. *Much safer than our window,* I thought. After a few beats, Kathy came out of the office and introduced herself. She was about five feet, five inches tall, thin, and had short, blonde, spiked hair. She was slightly older than I and had been the municipal clerk for Madisen for about fifteen years.

"I really appreciate your hospitality," I said to her.

"We are happy to be of help. We fared better than you in the storm and I'm terribly sorry for the devastation that your town suffered."

She walked me back down the corridor, toward the main entrance, and through to another wing of the building. The all-purpose room was a large area with white speckled linoleum floor and white walls. There were two banquet tables and numerous chairs.

"We can get you additional tables and chairs if you'd like and you are welcome to our copier," Kathy said.

"This is wonderful, thank you," I replied.

"Bathrooms are down the hallway and there is a kitchen area near the bathrooms," she informed me before she left.

A few minutes later, Bonnie arrived. "What do you need me to do?" she asked.

I put Bonnie in charge of incoming calls then I used my personal cell phone to dial out. I called Rodney to ask for a list of items that they needed. Next, I called our IT department to retrieve the password for the town's Facebook page.

I turned on my iPad and connected to Facebook. I put up a post on Sunshine's page: *Sunshine and its neighboring communities were nearly destroyed by last week's storm. Crews are working around the clock to reopen the island, but we need your help. We need shovels, bleach, and buckets. Please deliver to the Madisen Township Municipal Building, located at 478 Broad Street.*

Almost immediately, people were hitting "like" on the post and commenting on it, asking if there was anything else that was needed.

I called Rodney back and asked him if he thought anything else was needed. Bottled water or coffee? Volunteers? I posted another status update: *The crews on the island are in need of bottled water, gasoline containers, hand sanitizer, tarps, and work gloves. Please deliver to the Madisen Township Municipal Building.*

• • •

I couldn't believe my eyes when I arrived at Madisen's all-purpose room the next morning. The room was filled with supplies. Madisen's public works division took the liberty of moving items that were left outside indoors for me and I was extremely appreciative. There was more than I'd be able to carry. I was amazed at the generosity of others. I called Rodney and told him that I needed help getting supplies over the bridge into Sunshine. Within an hour, a group of Sunshine's employees arrived with hand trucks and they carted the goods off to their vehicles.

I learned from Rodney that the crews were able to clear out the main roads from the causeway to the municipal building in Sunshine. They would be working on as many side streets as possible in the upcoming days. Residents would not be allowed onto the island for the time being, but emergency personnel would now be able to cross over the bridge. I asked him what else was needed.

Rodney reported they could use more bottled water, first aid kits, and snacks. I posted the information on

Facebook once more. Again, the outpouring of help was overwhelming. People were stopping in the municipal building all day long. I was running out of room and Bonnie and I couldn't handle sorting everything. Additionally, I had an election to prepare for. I knew I needed help. I quickly put out another post: *Volunteers are needed to help sort and transport supplies for the Town of Sunshine. Please come to the Madisen Township Municipal Building.*

Eleven volunteers were recruited from the Facebook post. I turned over the job of handling supplies to them and I got busy with all the last-minute election details. I called the county board of elections and asked them to deliver the poll books to my temporary office in Madisen Township. I double-checked with the church that was housing our emergency polling location to make sure the voting machines were delivered. I called the poll workers to provide them with directions on where to pick up the poll books and where to report to work. The polls opened at six in the morning and poll workers were required to report at five fifteen a.m. I put out posts about where and when to vote and I notified the newspapers about our emergency setup.

According to the county clerk's office, there were already a large number of people taking advantage of early voting. Early voting isn't typically permissible in New Jersey, but the Governor created an executive order to grant it this year due to the dire circumstances we were facing. I created my spreadsheet for the election tallies and included an extra column for the early votes.

The only thing that bothered me about the election was Mayor O'Donnell. I found it outrageous that she didn't step down as mayor and that she continued to campaign for her reelection despite her arrest. I kept my fingers crossed that she wouldn't win her bid for reelection. I didn't know her opponent. He was a newcomer to the Town of Sunshine. The only requirements to run for office were that a candidate had to be a resident for one year and a registered voter. Alexander Phillips had moved into town just over a year ago. He was an Independent candidate and he filed his petitions on the day of the Primary Election, back in June, prior to my return from maternity leave. I had hoped that the voters read the newspapers and would think better than to vote for a corrupt politician like Frita.

• • •

On Monday morning, the supplies for the polling places arrived. The county decided to combine the four districts of Sunshine into two districts. That meant I had only two sets of poll books to be picked up and eight poll workers. Rose Sciaratta and Giuseppe Fruscione had volunteered to do the pickups for the two districts.

Giuseppe arrived first.

"Hiya there, Chelsey!" he said.

"Hey, Giuseppe. How did you make out in the storm?"

"Oh, Chelsey. I had a terrible time. I decided to ride it out. I never thought it would be so bad. My family was worried about my staying at home so my grandson, Roberto, came to stay with me. At some point during the night, after I fell asleep, Roberto came and woke me up. The water had risen and filled the downstairs of my house. He told me we had to get to the attic. He pulled me up the small ladder. I couldn't have gotten up there without him. Then he broke a hole in the roof and he carried me up another ladder to the outside. We waited for three hours on the roof until a helicopter came and rescued us."

"Oh, Giuseppe! I'm so sorry! How horrible! I had no idea!" I gave him a hug. "I'm so happy you're okay!"

"I'm okay because of my grandson. I owe him my life. I would have drowned if it wasn't for him." He started to cry. "My home is gone."

I felt so bad for him. I asked him if there was anything I could do for him. He was a proud man and he wouldn't accept anything from me. He told me he had a large family that was taking care of him.

"Ah, my grandkids will help rebuild the house if they know what's good for them. It's their inheritance," he said.

I helped Giuseppe out to his car with the poll supplies and I told him I'd stop in to check on him at the church in the morning.

Rose came in shortly after Giuseppe left. I asked her how she made out with the storm. She had stayed with her daughter during the storm, but didn't know the condition of her apartment yet. I hadn't seen the apartment complex when I was on the island, but I had heard it was in fairly good shape. I let her know.

"No worries," Rose said. "I hate my landlord. This was the kick in the bum I needed to get out of there and get moving. I'm going to look for a place near my daughter."

"You're moving out of Sunshine?" I asked.

"Yeah, I think it's time. There's a nice senior citizens' community near my daughter. I think I'd like it there."

"I'm going to miss you, Rose!"

I also walked her out to the car to help her with the supplies. When I returned, Bonnie informed me that Rodney called with the announcement that residents would be permitted on the island today with some restrictions. The streets had been cleared of enough sand to allow cars on the island.

I took the message from her and quickly put out a Facebook post: *Residents will be allowed into Sunshine Township today from noon until five p.m. Residents must bring a photo ID and proof of residence in order to gain entry. One vehicle per household will be permitted. It should be noted there is still no electricity or gas on the island.*

I called my parents and told them the news. I was sure they would want to drive to their house today to check on its condition and gather some of their belongings.

"If you want to check on your house, you can go ahead. I have enough volunteers to help me with phones and supplies," I said to Bonnie.

"What's the point? I have no downstairs to my home and have no way of getting to the upstairs of my house to get my things. I might as well stay here. I'd much rather answer all the 'where do I go to vote calls' than sit in front of my home and cry," she responded.

"The causeway will be backed up for miles anyway, with the military stopping each car to check IDs," I told her in an attempt to let her know I thought she was doing the right thing by not going to see the ruins.

At the end of the day, I decided to take a ride home to check on the status of the electricity. I unlocked the front door, then flicked on the light switch and *voilà*, it worked. I was ecstatic! I could move back into my house. But then it occurred to me, if I moved back in, I wouldn't have a baby sitter, since my parents' house was not currently inhabitable. I only had a two-bedroom home—there was my room and Mandy's room. After working out some details in my head, I called my parents. My mother sounded upset.

"Mom? Are you okay?" I asked.

"It's just seeing the house today. I know we were a lot luckier than some people. We didn't lose everything, but it was a lot to take in."

"How long will it take to get the insurance money?"

"The insurance company said there is a long wait list. They have tons of claims. There's no telling when we'll see some money. It won't pay for everything anyway. We'll need to hire some people to come out and gut the downstairs. Your father and I are just too old to do it."

"I have a suggestion."

"I'm all ears."

"I just got electricity back in my house. I was thinking about sleeping on a cot in Mandy's room and giving you and Dad my room. It would help us both out. You and Dad wouldn't have to drive over an hour each way to get back and forth to your home while you're having it repaired and I would have someone to watch Mandy without having to drive more than an hour back and forth to work."

"I like the idea. I'll just run it past your father to make sure."

"Do you mind if I stay here for the night? I have to be at work by five tomorrow morning and if I stay here, I won't have to leave the house before four a.m."

"That's fine. Mandy is just fine staying here."

"Feel free to move in tomorrow when I'm at work if Dad's fine with it. I won't get home until close to ten tonight. I can't leave until the polls close, the results are tallied, and I take the hand-written ballots back to the county."

"We'll probably see you tomorrow," my mom said.

# 22

At four o'clock in the morning, I jumped into the shower. It was so nice to be in my own shower, in my own home. I missed my little peanut, though. Today was going to be a rough day. I drove over to the church in Madisen first to put out signs and see how the poll workers were making out. Bonnie would always say that our workers were so old that their spouses were already collecting survivors' benefits. It was only five o'clock and they were already setting up. They might have been ancient, but they were incredibly reliable. I reminded them to start up the machines and open the doors to the public promptly at six.

I then headed over to the all-purpose room to man the phones. The main calls for today were people wanting to know how to get to the emergency poll location and when people would be allowed on the island again.

Bonnie arrived to help me at nine in the morning. I ran out at ten to buy donuts and coffee for the poll workers. When I arrived at the polls, I noticed that a reporter from the *Lagoon Tribune* was doing exit polling. Out of curiosity, I asked her what the polls were predicting. She said it was a close race, to my dismay. I dropped off the donuts and coffee and took a long lunch to reenergize myself. I headed back to my makeshift office around two o'clock so that Bonnie could take a breather as well.

When Bonnie returned, I headed back out to the church. The poll workers reported it was slow all day. I hoped the polls would pick up during the evening hours, when the nine-to-fivers were on their way home from work.

As the close of polls neared, I found myself biting my nails. I was a nervous wreck waiting for the results. I wanted to be rid of Frita O'Donnell as soon as possible, and not having to work with her was a start. There was no date selected for her trial yet and I didn't want to wait for a trial and sentencing for her to be out of my life for good.

The fax machine rang at eight thirty and I got a taste of the preliminary results. The write-in and early voting ballots were tallied with Frita winning by only ten votes.

"Nuts!" I said.

"What? What's the matter?" Bonnie asked.

"I have the county's tallies and they are showing Frita winning by ten votes."

"That doesn't mean she won."

"It's usually a good indication of the winner," I told Bonnie. It was the truth. In every election I had worked in this job and my former job, the write-in results mirrored the machine results. The winner of the write-ins was always the winner.

I was on the edge of my seat waiting for Rose and Giuseppe to come to my office with the machine votes.

"I predict Rose will be here by eight forty-seven," Bonnie said.

"I'll take Giuseppe by eight forty-two," I said.

It was a little game we decided to play to pass the time tonight—predicting who would be the first poll worker to bring us results and what time. I was the closest; Giuseppe arrived at eight forty-five. We had a system where I checked in the poll supplies to make sure everything was signed properly, the machine keys were returned, the machine cartridges were sealed, and the written ballots were properly handled. Bonnie would take the result print outs from each machine and enter them into a spreadsheet so that we had a final tally.

When Bonnie finished the tally, she breathed a sigh of relief.

"Well? Don't keep me waiting any longer!" I said impatiently.

"New guy won," Bonnie announced.

"Are you messing with me?"

"Nope, new guy won by a little under a hundred votes."

I did a little victory dance and Bonnie laughed. As of January 1st, whether or not Frita was put away for her crimes, she would no longer be my boss! I couldn't have felt more overjoyed at the moment.

We finished up our work for the evening, and I drove to the county to deliver the written votes. I arrived at home to see my parents' car in the driveway. I smiled; I was glad they decided to stay with me and I couldn't wait to see my precious baby girl.

I went inside and told my parents the good news about Frita not winning tonight, then I crept into Mandy's room to sleep next to her. She looked like a peaceful little angel in her crib. I drifted off to sleep, listening to the sounds of her breathing.

• • •

The day after the election, Frita showed up in the Madisen Township all-purpose room where I was working. I picked up my cell phone and dialed 9-1-1. She was screaming, "You rigged the election, you little rat! I am going to kill you!"

I backed away from her, but she kept coming at me, yelling and carrying on like a lunatic. I grabbed my purse, reached in, and pulled out the pepper spray Bonnie had given me. I depressed the pump and shot her in the eyes with the spray. She shrieked and rubbed her eyes. "You witch!" she hollered. Within minutes, Madisen Township police officers showed up. I handed them a copy of my restraining order, which I always carried with me, and they placed her under arrest for violating the order.

The officers dragged her out in handcuffs as she kept yelling, "I'm going to call the attorney general; you rigged the election. I'm going to get you, Chelsey Alton!"

I thought, *Be my guest!* I yelled back at her as they dragged her out the door, "There is no way I could have rigged that election and if you have to tell yourself that in order to accept your fate, then so be it." That was a woman who was in total denial.

Madisen's clerk came into the room. "I'm just checking to see if everyone's okay," Kathy said.

"We're fine now, thanks! You probably aren't going to ever invite us back with all the drama we brought today," I said to her.

"Are you kidding? This was the highlight of my week! Nothing ever goes on here. I was excited for a change!" she said.

We all laughed.

"You're definitely working the council meeting tomorrow for me, right?" I asked Bonnie.

"I will, but I'd much rather see you have to work the meeting, so I can watch you pepper spray that bitch again!"

I was relieved that Bonnie would handle the meeting for me. I didn't know how that would work out anyway if I was supposed to work the meeting. I'm sure Colby would have directed me to stay away from the meeting, given the circumstances and the restraining order.

I asked Bonnie to text me after the meeting to see how it went. The resolution to officially reappoint Bonnie as the deputy town clerk was on the agenda and I was eager to know if it passed without issues. She later told me it did.

• • •

The remainder of November and most of December were dedicated to cleaning up the Municipal Complex and putting the office back together. Rodney hired a contractor to drain the flood waters from the basement of the municipal building, gut it, and handle mold remediation. The ground floor offices were in decent condition and didn't need much work. Replacement windows were installed in one afternoon.

Bonnie and I spent a lot of time taking in donations, coordinating volunteers and helping those in need get back on their feet. The range of support and donations we received to give out to the community was astonishing.

Even though we were all working hard, Sunshine wouldn't be completely back to normal for a long, long time. Streets were littered with drenched carpeting, rotting drywall, mold-infested furniture, and inoperable major appliances. Garbage haulers were working overtime in an attempt to clear all the debris. Utility companies were providing around the clock teams to restore power to the community. Crews were removing fallen trees and limbs for weeks. The public works department was desperately trying to rebuild dunes that had washed away in the storm in an effort to protect the town from any winter storms that might come our way. Most residents were unable to inhabit their homes and the majority of those who worked in Sunshine lost their livelihood.

The large dunes near the Municipal Complex protected the buildings in the complex and I knew I was lucky to have a home and a paycheck coming in. I actually felt sorry for Mr. Triggers. He had lost everything, which was his greatest fear. It was like he had a sixth sense about something like this happening and it made him extremely passionate about trying to save his home in advance.

By Thanksgiving, not too many Sunshine residents had a lot to be thankful for. Rebuilding had begun for only half of the homeowners and businesses in town. My parents were still living with me and I liked having them around. They had a way of making me feel safe and secure. They loved being around Mandy 24/7 too, but they would have liked to be back in their own home.

A contractor had begun working on their house earlier in the week. He estimated that renovations would be done by Christmas. With my parents around all the time lately, it made me realize I wanted a big family of my own. I was done with my independent phase. I realized that life was too short and could be taken away easily. I wanted to share my life with someone special and have a happy home, much like the home my parents provided me with growing up.

# 23

December 21st. Today was supposed to be the end of the world, according to those who believed in the Mayan calendar doomsday predictions. It seemed like the end of the world when Mr. Triggers showed up at the window. Bonnie and I were about to exchange our Christmas presents when he arrived and put a damper on the holiday spirit.

"I want to see the mayor now!" he demanded.

"Perhaps you'd like to wait until after the first of the year when the new mayor takes office," I said.

Mr. Triggers turned around without saying a word and walked away. His face showed no expression.

"That was weird," I said to Bonnie.

"Sure was," she said.

We opened our presents. Bonnie had bought me a cashmere sweater, scarf, and hat.

"I wish you wouldn't spend so much money!" I said to her. "Thank you very much!"

I had bought Bonnie a gift card to Woody's for dinner. I never knew what to buy for a woman who has it all.

Or should I say, *had* it all before the storm. I didn't know what she needed, but I thought being able to take a break from renovations and going to dinner would be something she would enjoy.

"I was going to buy you paint so you can change your house color again, but since you now need new siding anyway, my idea was a bad one."

We both laughed.

"Thank you," she said to me. "This is perfect. I love Woody's."

I went to the kitchen and made myself some coffee. After settling in at my desk with my hazelnut decaf and opening up my emails, I heard the unthinkable. *Pop, pop, pop, scream.* I ran to my office door and saw Bonnie lying on the floor covered in blood. She glanced at me, then at the window, and she closed her eyes. I heard the crack of the office door being kicked in, but could not see it from where I was standing. I panicked, but thought enough to run to the back office, where Rodney happened to be and lock the door. He looked at me in horror.

"What is going on?"

I couldn't speak. All the blood drained out of my face and my hands shook uncontrollably. I picked up the phone and dialed 9-1-1.

*Pop, pop, pop.*

"9-1-1, what is your emergency?"

More shots rang out; more screams of terror could be heard.

"Someone is shooting, Bonnie was shot, please hurry," was all that I could manage to say. There was a loud bang, then the door to the back office burst open. We found ourselves staring at Robert Triggers, all decked out in military fatigues, holding a rifle in his hand, and with at least two guns in holsters at his sides. He had shot through the door lock, then kicked in the remaining door. I froze. Rodney gasped. Triggers' angry voice boomed.

"PUT...THE...PHONE...DOWN!"

I could hear the dispatcher saying, "Are you hurt? Hello? Are you there?"

I slowly placed the receiver back on the hook. I could hear Rodney whisper, *"Please."* I couldn't move. I couldn't speak. I was trembling and my heart was pounding so wildly I could feel the pounding in my head.

"SIT!" he demanded.

With his gun aimed directly at me, we both slowly took a seat.

Sirens blared in the distance. Mr. Triggers made his way over to the window to look out, then he closed the blinds.

I was thinking to myself, *Can I run for the door?* Probably not, I was shaking too hard and I didn't think I'd be able to outrun the gun. Rodney looked like he could faint at any moment. I supposed that no amount of marijuana would make someone feel calm enough to get through this.

Triggers was silent for what seemed to be an eternity. I could hear the commotion outside with police cars, but I couldn't see what was going on since the blinds were closed. I felt a little relieved that the police were here and that they probably knew Triggers had us, due to my 9-1-1 call, but I still couldn't help the feeling of dread that poured over me. My mind wandered to my daughter, and how I would soon be dead. How I wouldn't be able to see her grow up. How she wouldn't remember me telling her I loved her, how she wouldn't remember anything about me. How she would have to grow up without a mom.

*My poor parents,* I thought. Having their daughter die and having to raise their grandchild. How they would have to explain one day what happened to her mommy. I choked back my sobs. *Don't cry, Chelsey, don't cry. He's more likely to shoot if you cry.*

Triggers finally broke his silence. "I want my dunes and YOU are going to help me get them!" He glared at me. I remained silent. I didn't know what to say.

"DID...YOU...HEAR...ME?!"

I whispered, "Yes."

I wasn't sure why he still wanted his dunes at this point. His house was gone. But, we were talking about someone with a gun; chances are, he wasn't thinking clearly.

The phone started to ring. Rodney and I glanced toward the phone, then toward Triggers.

"DON'T answer that."

We sat silently. Triggers started pacing. The phone continued to ring. He started banging his forehead with the palm of his hand and repeating, "Think, think."

Rodney said he could answer the phone. Triggers screamed at him, telling him to shut up. The phone stopped ringing.

"YOU!" he shouted, pointing his finger at me. "You call public works and tell them to make arrangements right now to have dunes installed OR ELSE!"

I normally don't think very quickly on my feet and maybe it was more of a survival instinct than anything, but I picked up the phone and dialed 555-2400, which was the non-emergency police number. I prayed that Triggers couldn't hear it when the voice on the other line said, "Sunshine Police, Dispatcher Forty-one."

"Hi, it's Chelsey. I need you to make arrangements to install dunes on Fourth Street."

Detective Texidoro picked up the phone. I almost started to cry again when I heard his voice.

"Chelsey, it's Tex. Good job. You are going to be fine, just stay calm. Now, can you tell us who is there with you?"

"Rodney is here and he can approve the purchase order for sand for the dunes. Can you please make the arrangements?"

"Is Robert Triggers there with you?"

I guess it wasn't that hard to figure out that Triggers was the nut case that kept asking for the dunes.

"Chelsey, can you tell me how many guns he has?"

"Three truck loads of sand would be good for starters."

"Three guns? Are they machine guns?

"No."

"Hand guns or shot guns?"

I could see Triggers, seemingly irate, telling me to wrap it up. "Yes! If you could put a rush on it, that would be good. Thanks, bye." I quickly hung up the phone.

Unknown to us, there was a huge gathering outside. Flashing lights from emergency vehicles filled the parking lot. Police crime scene tape encircled the building, creating a boundary between law enforcement and curious onlookers. SWAT teams and FBI agents set up an emergency command station at the senior center. Various news vans were arriving.

Reporters holding microphones and cameramen with headsets were awaiting information that could be released on air.

My thoughts turned to Bonnie. Was she alive or perhaps badly injured? I pleaded with God to let her live. She had two young children and didn't deserve to die. Could the EMTs get to her or were they afraid it wasn't safe for them to enter the building? I kept praying until the phone rang again. Triggers told me to answer it.

"Hello?"

"Chelsey? This is Agent Salvatore Romeo of the FBI. I will be acting as your hostage negotiator. Please see if Mr. Triggers will take the phone."

I motioned toward Triggers. "They want to talk to you."

"Tell them I have nothing to talk about."

I relayed the message.

"Ask him if he has any demands," Romeo said.

I asked.

Mr. Triggers flipped out. He began screaming and carrying on like a maniac. "Do I have any demands? Do I have any demands?" He grabbed the phone out of my hand and screamed into it, "I want my dunes and get me that wench Frita O'Donnell while you are at it!"

He slammed the receiver down and grabbed the entire phone, violently ripping it out of the wall, then slamming it to the ground. He then jumped on it and kicked it clear across the room.

Rodney and I traded glances. We were both terrified and we sat there silently. I found myself holding my breath from time to time. I was afraid to exhale. Triggers started pacing and smacking his head with his hand again.

"We are going to stay here until I have dunes installed and until Frita O'Donnell shows her ugly face," Triggers said.

"How will you know when the dunes are installed?" Rodney asked.

"Good point," Triggers said. He pointed the gun directly into Rodney's face, aiming it between his eyes. "Is there a TV in here?"

"In my office," Rodney hesitantly replied.

"Let's go," Triggers said, motioning toward the door with the gun.

He marched us at gunpoint out of the back office. When we reached Bonnie's desk, I saw a large smear of blood on the floor where I last saw her lying. It appeared as if someone had dragged her out. I couldn't control myself as I let out a whimper.

"SHUT THE HELL UP!" Triggers screamed. "I killed her and I'll kill you too."

He told us to move into the lobby. The floors and walls were covered in blood. There were three people lying dead. I had never seen anything so gruesome in my life. They didn't look like any of the employees of Sunshine. I assumed they were residents doing business in the town. It was sickening to know these poor innocent individuals had met their fate as a result of this madman by being in the wrong place at the wrong time. I silently wondered if Bonnie made it out, since I didn't see her body anywhere.

Through the glass doors, I could see a S.W.A.T. team with guns pointed directly into the building. "Hold your fire," was shouted by someone I couldn't see.

Triggers grabbed Rodney and used him as a human shield to get through the lobby and down the hallway to Rodney's office. Inside Rodney's office, I was instructed to turn on the TV. We were all over the news. The volume on the TV was down, so Triggers instructed me to turn it up.

Video of the municipal building surrounded by law enforcement was streaming. The reporter was saying that police had reported a hostage situation. My Facebook photo flashed across the screen and the fact that I was a confirmed hostage in the situation was announced. I thought that was pretty darn quick that the reporters already got my picture off of Facebook.

"Sit down!" Triggers yelled.

I jumped out of my skin. For a split second when I was watching TV, I had zoned out. I swiftly scrambled into the closest chair. We sat there for a couple of hours without saying anything. Rodney's phone started to ring. Triggers told me to answer it.

"Town of Sunshine," I said. It was a force of habit to answer the phones that way. It was someone trying to sell me a copier. I hung the phone up and said, "Sales call." My thoughts turned toward the phone. I so badly wanted to call my parents and hear my daughter's babble. I didn't want to leave this world without telling her I loved her one last time. I wanted my last words on this Earth to be, "I love you, baby girl." I began to think I had nothing to lose.

"Mr. Triggers, sir. I was wondering if I could call my daughter and say good-bye to her."

"No," he said in a booming voice.

"She's only ten months old and if you're going to kill me, I would like to say good-bye to her." A tear fell from my eye.

"A ten-month-old baby?" he asked.

"Yes," I said softly with my eyes cast downward.

"So that *was* you in the grocery store!" he exclaimed.

Oh lord. I had forgotten I told that lie and now it was coming back to bite me. I wasn't quite as clever as I had thought.

"Grocery store?" I asked.

"Yes, you're just another lying bitch!" he yelled.

I panicked, but thought enough to say, "Is that where you had run into my sister? You told me you met my twin sister. Was her daughter with her with her when you saw her?"

He looked sufficiently befuddled. He sat silently for a little while, staring at me. I was getting jittery. I wasn't sure if he was buying it.

"Fine," he said to my surprise. "You have one minute to make your call."

Oh, thank heavens; he bought it. I picked up the phone and quickly dialed my parents' number. *Please pick up, please pick up* was going through my head. I finally heard my mother's voice. "Hello?"

"Mom?" I said in a shaky voice.

"Chelsey, oh my god, I'm watching the news, are you okay? Did he hurt you?"

I took a deep breath. "Mom, please go get Mandy. I need to tell her I love her."

My mother let out a wail and burst into tears. My face was red, trying to hold back my own tears until I was done on the phone.

"Thirty seconds," Triggers said.

"Please, Mom, quickly, I only have thirty seconds."

"The phone is near her ear," my mother said.

"Mandy, baby, Mommy loves you with all my heart. You be a good girl for Grandmom and Grandpop. I love you, baby girl."

I could hear Mandy say, "Ba ba." That's all she was able to say at her age, besides some other babbling.

I broke down in tears as I hung up the phone. I could no longer control my sobs.

"Why are you doing this?" Rodney asked softly. I could see the Rodney's hands were trembling and he was sweating bullets. He looked like he was in bad shape. I figured he was way past due for his medications.

Mr. Triggers grew incensed. "Why am I doing this? Why am I doing this?" he shouted. "I'm doing this because you people messed up my whole life. You screwed me."

"How?" Rodney asked. I thought this was rather bold of Rodney. I feared Rodney was going to push this guy over the edge and the gun would start firing. My hopes of getting out alive were bleak, but I still felt there was a slim chance of someone saving us. If Triggers started shooting now, our chances would be gone. I quickly butted in and said, "What he means is, what can we do to help you?"

"You could've installed the dunes before the freakin' storm took away everything I owned; that is what you could have done, but now it's too late!" Triggers said in a very evil tone. "You took away my life and now I'm going to take away yours, but not before I make that Frita O'Donnell pay for all her red tape!"

"The mayor took your life away, not us. She tried to take my life away too. I'd be happy to see you make her pay," I said.

I was trying to keep him focused on a different target. I hated the mayor, so why not keep his attention there? It was a fat chance he'd ever get to her after this hostage stunt, so I didn't feel like I was putting another person in harm's way by saying that.

"Yeah, she did destroy my life," he said. "But you work for her, so you are against me too."

"No I'm not," I said. "I hate her. She put me in jail for no reason."

It was time to break my rules about being professional to those outside of my inner circle, and it worked. It finally got his attention. Maybe if he felt I could empathize with him, he would let me go.

"What do you mean?" he said.

"She falsely accused me of stealing and embezzlement. She made the police arrest me. I got thrown into jail. I got fired. I had to post bail and hire an attorney. I had no money to pay my bills. Then she tried to have me killed. Sent two goons after me. Tried to take my poor baby girl's mother away. I have a restraining order against her."

"See! I knew she was evil. She ruins people's lives."

"She does, but she is going to get hers. She was arrested for being the leader in an identity theft ring."

"Then why did I see her yesterday at the pharmacy?"

"She didn't have her day in court yet, but she will. She will be behind bars for a long time."

Mr. Triggers was silent. I didn't know if I still had him relating to me or if I was losing him. It was around noontime. I couldn't think of anything else to say about the mayor. I had to pee really badly.

"Would I be permitted to go to the bathroom?" I asked.

Mr. Triggers scowled at me.

"You and Rodney could come into the room. There are stalls on the bathroom doors inside, but you'd be able to see my feet and see I wasn't running away. I promise, I'll be quick."

"I need to go too," Rodney said.

"Fine," Triggers said. He motioned to us with the gun to move out of the room.

He led us to the bathroom and we both took a stall to do our business, while Triggers waited watchfully in the doorway. I thought the fact that he let us use the restroom was a good sign. Maybe he would let us live too. We washed our hands and Triggers led us back into Rodney's office at gunpoint.

Rodney's phone rang again. Triggers told me to answer it. The voice from the other end said, "Chelsey, this is Agent Romeo again. Is Mr. Triggers willing to talk yet?"

I looked at Triggers. "They want to know if you want to talk yet."

"No!" Triggers screamed.

"He doesn't wish to speak at this time. Is there any message?" I asked.

"Has he hurt either one of you?" Romeo asked.

"No."

"Has he told you his demands?"

"He wants his dunes installed and he is watching the TV to see that it's accomplished. He also wants Frita O'Donnell down here."

"Hang the phone up," Triggers shouted.

"He wanted to know if we had demands," I said. I purposely included the "we" in that sentence, because I wanted Triggers to think I was on his side. I had nothing left to lose.

"They know my demands," Triggers replied.

"Yes, but we should ask for more. Like food. Are you hungry? I could go for a pizza."

"Yeah, okay, fine. Food."

I picked up the phone and dialed the non-emergency police number. I wasn't sure how to reach Agent Romeo, but I assumed they would be on the police lines. I knew the non-emergency line was a recorded line, so if Romeo wasn't reachable this way, he would still be able to replay the tapes. I was surprised when Romeo answered. I assumed since they could see where the call was coming from, they knew it was us.

"Agent Salvatore Romeo."

"There's another demand," I said.

"I'm listening."

"Pizza and soda please."

"Are you and Rodney hurt?"

"No."

"We will leave the food outside of the door. Try to get Triggers to pick up the food himself."

"Understood."

I told Triggers the food would arrive in twenty minutes. It was close to two o'clock in the afternoon when the food arrived. Triggers insisted I go to get the food. He threatened to kill Rodney if I didn't come back. There was no way I was going to be able to convince Triggers to get the food like Agent Romeo asked and I wasn't about to risk my life by trying.

I made my way out of Rodney's office and into the lobby. I moved slowly, stepping over a body and tiptoeing through pools of blood until I reached the main doors. I could see all the police cars and commotion outside. I slowly opened the doors. I heard a voice yell, "Hold your fire."

I held the door open just wide enough to grasp the pizza box. Two men wearing dark tactical gear ran toward me from the sides of the building, but stayed along the siding, away from the glass doors. One shouted to me, "Are you okay?"

I pulled the food into the municipal building without answering him. I didn't want Triggers to hurt Rodney, so I wasn't about to say anything that would cast doubts in Triggers' mind that I would return. I hurried down the hallway and into Rodney's office. Triggers ate in silence. He indicated that Rodney and I could eat. I forced myself to take a couple of bites. I didn't have an appetite, but I knew I needed to keep my strength up in case an opportunity to run presented itself.

Rodney spoke up after a while. "Why don't you let Chelsey go? She is a single mom and her child needs her. You can keep me and still get what you need by holding me hostage," he said to Triggers.

Triggers looked at him for a very long time without saying anything. I spoke up. "You should let Rodney go instead of me. Rodney has a terminal illness and is going to die anyway. You'd be more likely to get your dunes if you have a young, single woman that you are holding hostage."

"What are you doing?" Rodney whispered. "Your daughter needs you."

I was torn. I knew my daughter needed me, but I thought I could talk my way out of the situation better than Rodney could. I felt that if Rodney stayed, Triggers would definitely kill him and Rodney looked worse than I had ever seen him at this point. He was sweaty and twitching. He needed medical attention and I felt I had a better chance of making it out alive. I was torn between doing what was right and doing what was right for me. I chose to do the right thing.

"Mr. Triggers, you could bargain with them. Tell them that in exchange for three truckloads of sand being deposited at the end of your street, you will let one of us go."

Mr. Triggers still sat silently. He seemed to be pondering the idea.

"Get them on the phone," Triggers said.

I dialed the number. Romeo answered again. Triggers told me to tell them the bargain.

"He has a proposition for you," I said.

"Put him on the phone," Romeo said.

"They want to talk to you," I said to Mr. Triggers.

Triggers shook his head. "They talk to you or no deal."

"He won't get on the phone and he said he won't provide this offer again."

"I'm listening," Romeo said.

"Mr. Triggers would like three truckloads of sand delivered to the end of his street. Once the loads are delivered, he will release one of us."

"Tell him to release one of you now and we'll consider the offer."

I relayed the message. Triggers would not allow it and told me to hang up. I hung up the phone like I was told. I felt hopeless. We sat without speaking for the next several hours. The sun was starting to set. It was getting dark. Triggers did not want the lights on. It was growing darker and darker. I had to pee again, but was afraid to ask.

"Would you consider letting us go?" I finally asked.

"No," Mr. Triggers said. "Not until I get my dunes and I get my revenge on Bitch-face O'Donnell. If it takes days or weeks, then we'll be here for days or weeks."

The only hope I thought we'd have was if Triggers fell asleep and we were somehow able to sneak out. I didn't have a choice but to wait it out.

By ten p.m., the day had taken its toll on me. I was spent. I didn't have an ounce of energy left. I wanted to close my eyes and fall asleep, but my nerves wouldn't let me take even a small catnap. Mr. Triggers was sitting behind Rodney's desk and he had kicked his feet up. At the moment he put his head back and I thought he had dozed off, I saw a small red light appear on his neck. I looked around to see where the light was coming from. It appeared to be coming from the small square window in the door to Rodney's office. I squinted my eyes in an attempt to see better in the dark, but I couldn't tell what was making the light appear.

A moment later, Mr. Triggers lifted his head and the small, round, red light appeared in the middle of his forehead. It was then that I recalled seeing such a light many times on TV and in the movies. I sunk down into my seat and closed my eyes as tightly as I could. My heart started pounding in my chest. I thought, *Please don't miss.*

With a single shot, a sharpshooter took out Mr. Triggers with a hit between his eyes. My ordeal was over. Mr. Triggers was dead. Law enforcement rushed into the room, grabbing Rodney and me by the arms, and escorting us swiftly out of the municipal building. It all happened so fast. I was thankful it was still dark in the room when they pulled us out. I didn't want to see the gory scene that was left behind. Rodney and I were taken to an ambulance, wrapped up in blankets, and given a once-over. Within a few minutes, I saw my mother being escorted by an officer through the police caution tape. My father was a few steps behind.

I stood up and collapsed into my mother's arms. Dad came up and embraced the two of us tightly. We all cried.

"Where's Mandy?" I asked.

My mother took my face in her hands, and wiped the tears from my cheeks. "She's fine," she said. "She's with your cousins, Daisy and James. They drove here when they heard the news."

"Bonnie?" I asked while I sobbed. "Is she dead?"

"Bonnie was in surgery last we heard, to remove a bullet," my father reported.

"I want to go to the hospital. I need to see if she's okay."

My parents didn't argue with me. They knew I had been through an ordeal like never before. My father wrapped his arms around me and walked me over to where they were parked. He drove directly to the hospital.

I saw Jayce immediately in the waiting area. He looked distraught. I walked up to him with tears streaming down my eyes. He hugged me and started to cry.

"Is she okay?" I asked with my voice shaking.

"She's still sleeping off the anesthesia, but she's going to make it," he said. "She was shot in the shoulder and chest. She managed to drag herself out of the building to safety. It was touch and go there for a while. Her lung collapsed. She lost a lot of blood."

Bonnie was in the ICU, so we were not permitted in to see her. I told Jayce to give her my love and tell her I was concerned. I wiped my tears on my sleeve, then I gave him another big hug. My parents drove me back to their house. I immediately checked in on Mandy. Normally, I wouldn't want to wake her, but I had to hold her in my arms. I lifted her from her crib and carried her to the rocking chair. I gave her a little kiss on the head and said, "Mommy loves Mandy."

She looked up at me with her big eyes and said, "Ba ba." Her tiny eyelids closed and she nestled into my chest to fall back to sleep. I rocked her and cuddled her for over an hour.

After I put her back in her crib, I took the longest shower of my life. I couldn't get rid of the feeling that there was blood on my skin, even though I washed myself over and over. I also could not get the brutal images of Bonnie lying in a pool of her own blood and the dead bodies in the lobby out of my head.

I curled up in a ball on the shower floor and wept until I had no tears left. Then I crawled into bed and slept for two days.

# 24

*A* year had passed since the traumatic events in my life. Frita O'Donnell and Lorraine Paso were both found guilty during their trials and were sentenced to a very long time behind prison walls. It was stressful to testify against them, but my parents hung in there with me, encouraging me, making me feel less afraid.

Bonnie recovered from her injuries after a few long and difficult months. She eventually quit her job at Sunshine Township, as did I. Rodney had taken a disability retirement last I heard. I was trying to get on with my life.

It was Christmas morning and my almost two-year-old was opening the presents Santa left for her under the tree.

"You forgot one, Mandy. Let's go in the kitchen. Santa left another present for you in there."

Mandy ran into the kitchen. When she got there, she froze with her eyes wide and her smile even wider. Her present, complete with a big red bow, was wagging his tail and barking at her.

"Puppy!" she yelled.

"Yes, baby, that's your puppy. Santa brought him for you."

Santa partly brought him for me too. I wasn't afraid of my own shadow any longer, but I decided I wanted a family companion…and watchdog, anyway.

"He's a German Shepherd. What do you want to name him?"

"Snicues."

"Snickers? Okay, that's a good name."

The phone rang.

"Merry Christmas!" It was my mom.

"Merry Christmas, Mom. Mandy says Merry Christmas too!"

"How does she like the puppy?"

"She loves him! She named him Snickers."

"Are you coming over today?"

"We wouldn't miss it."

"Bring the dog."

I dressed Mandy in her pretty red and black dress.

"Pittie," she said.

"Yes, you are, sweetie. Mandy is very pretty," I told her.

I loved that she could talk now and communicate more with me. She was the center of my world. If it wasn't for her, I don't think I would have been able to make it through the post-traumatic stress. She gave me a reason to keep going, keep living. I had been in counseling for the past eleven months and my psychologist said I was ready to stop the sessions and get on with my life.

If there was any good that came out of my horrible experience of working at Sunshine, it was that I had gotten my wish. I was now a stay-at-home mom. Bonnie, Rodney, and I each won a $500,000.00 settlement from the town for their failure to maintain a secure working environment. This was plenty of money for me to be the full-time caretaker of Mandy until she was at the age to start school. Still, there was something missing. I wasn't sure what I wanted to do with my life. Did I want another job? Or to go back to school to study something else? Or to meet a nice man to date? There was a lot I needed to figure out.

We drove over the bridge to my parents' house. The island was starting to make a comeback from last year's dreadful storm. Many businesses were back up and running. Everything was starting to look bright and shiny new. Time heals all, I suppose.

"We're here!" I announced.

"Me-ma and Pa Pa?"

"Yes honey, we're at Mom Mom's and Pop Pop's house. I bet they have more presents for you!"

"Yay!"

My parents had finished their remodel of the entire downstairs six months ago. It was nice. They added granite countertops, hard wood floors, and top-of-the-line appliances. The smell of turkey and stuffing filled the air when we walked into the door.

"Smells good in here," I said.

My parents made a big fuss over Mandy in her dress and since the patience of a child her age isn't the greatest, they let her open her presents before dinner. We sat down to eat. I was barely able to spoon the mashed potatoes onto my plate when my mother started.

"You know, Chelsey, it's been a year."

"I know, Mom," I said with condescending tone.

"I know you don't want to hear this from me again, but you need to get out of the house and have a social life again."

"My psychologist says I'm fine."

"Yes, fine, but you don't have a life."

"I have a life. I have Mandy to worry about. And now I have a dog. That's all I need."

"I just wish you would take care of yourself too. Taking care of yourself doesn't mean you won't be taking good care of Mandy."

"I do take care of myself. I never missed a counseling session."

"You know what I mean. You don't go out with friends, you don't date, and you basically don't leave your house except to come here."

"I don't feel much like going out these days."

"You're not the same Chelsey that you were before the ordeal."

"I don't know if *that* Chelsey is ever coming back, Mom."

"We're just worried about you."

"Don't be."

"You know Jose and Stephanie are having a New Year's party. Why don't you and Mandy come?"

"Mandy goes to bed by eight and Snickers needs to be let out. You know I can't go to a New Year's party."

"The party starts at seven. You can bring the dog here and leave him in his crate. Just go for an hour," she pleaded. "If you are having a good time, then we'll take Mandy home with us and we'll take care of the dog so that you can stay and enjoy yourself."

"I don't know."

"You haven't seen any friends in a year. Getting out will do you good. Just go for an hour with us."

"If I say I'll go, will you leave me alone and never bring up this subject again?

"Yes, okay."

"Fine then, I'll go. I'll meet you here a little before seven."

• • •

I arrived at my parents' house at six forty-five on New Year's Eve. I decided to wear the little black dress that I had bought over a year ago when I went shopping with Bonnie. I never had a chance to wear it, so this seemed like a good occasion to dress up. I knew my parents were just looking out for me. I did want to get out and start enjoying myself again. It was time. I deserved to take pleasure in the little things again, like friends. I was nervous because I hadn't seen Tex since *that* day and I didn't want to discuss or think about Mr. Triggers ever again.

My father met me outside. I tried to hand the crate containing Snickers to him without messing up my dress. He put Snickers in the house for me so I didn't have to unbuckle Mandy. Five minutes later, my parents jumped in their car after giving Snickers some water and a treat. I followed them in my car to the party. Tex answered the door and gave me a giant hug. "We've missed you," he said.

"I've missed you too."

He took our coats and pointed us toward the food. I was relieved that Tex didn't say anything about Sunshine or the dreaded day I didn't wish to discuss. Mandy waddled over to play with another toddler who looked to be a year older than she was.

"Go ahead, go get something to eat, I'll keep an eye on her," my mother said to me.

My dad struck up a conversation with Tex and I headed toward the food. I poured myself a nice large glass of homemade sangria. I had forgotten how good Stephanie's sangria was. I checked over the delicacies on the table.

"The bratwurst is awesome," I heard a voice say.

I turned to look and there was a handsome man standing next to me with brown hair and hazel eyes. He was probably about my age, but had a cute, boyish appearance to him. "I'll have to try that," I said.

Stephanie called out, "Hey, Lance, your son is trying to eat the soap in the bathroom."

"I'll be right back," he said to me.

He chased after the three-year-old that my daughter had been playing with and then returned.

"Your son is adorable," I said. "That's my daughter he's playing with."

"Yup, that's my boy; already chasing the pretty girls."

I smiled. I looked at Lance's hand. No ring. Maybe this was going to be my lucky night. I spotted Bonnie running toward me.

"Chelsey!" she said. "I missed you so much!"

She gave me a huge embrace. "I missed you too!" I said.

I *had* missed Bonnie. I hadn't kept in touch with anyone too much after the ordeal I had been through. I didn't want to do much of anything except pay attention to my daughter. The moment I had thought I might never see Mandy again, I had made a promise, that if I had gotten out of that situation alive, I would spend every free moment of my time with her. As a result, I didn't spend much time maintaining my friendships. I knew I had to change this. I didn't want to become an overbearing, smothering parent. I was thrilled to reconnect with Bonnie and rekindle my previous friendships. I made a New Year's resolution to start a fresh new life in this upcoming year.

"Where's Jayce?" I asked.

"He's on call at the hospital tonight, so he couldn't come."

"That's a shame. Where are the kids?"

"They're with my in-laws."

Lance walked away to say hello to another couple walking in the door.

"Who's the hottie?" Bonnie asked.

"I don't know. I heard Stephanie call him 'Lance' but I haven't had a chance to talk to him much."

"I didn't see a ring on his finger."

"Neither did I and I haven't seen him with a date yet," I said. "It really is great to see you. How are you feeling?"

"Oh, I'm just fine, I'm all healed up, good as new."

Bonnie and I spent the next hour catching up. By that time, my parents were ready to take Mandy home with them.

I decided to stay and spend a little more time with Bonnie. I went over to say good-bye to my daughter. I gave her a big hug.

"Now you have fun at your sleep-over with Mom Mom and Pop Pop," I told her.

"Mandy loves Mommy," she said as she waved to me.

"And Mommy loves Mandy!" I said.

A few minutes later, the little boy ran up to me.

"Hi. What's your name?" he asked.

"I'm Chelsey; what's your name?"

"My name is Kris. Where did Mandy go?"

"Mandy had to go home to go to sleep."

"Are you her mommy?"

"Yes, honey, I'm her mommy."

"Will you be my mommy too?"

"Oh, sweetie, I don't think your mommy will like that very much. I'm sure she wants to be your only mommy."

"My mommy died."

My heart broke. I felt so bad for this little boy and I wasn't sure what to say.

"I'm so sorry, sweetie. You must miss your mommy very much."

"I'm looking for a new mommy."

"How about we play a game," I said, trying to lift his spirits and change the subject. We played with some toys for a little while, then he curled up in the corner of the couch and drifted off to sleep. I grabbed the afghan that was folded over the back of the couch, covered him with it, then tiptoed away. I hadn't eaten yet and the sangria was starting to go to my head.

I found Stephanie in the kitchen, putting out more food. I grabbed an appetizer.

"That's a mini Beef Wellington," Stephanie pointed out. Stephanie always outdid herself with food when she threw a party.

"It's delicious," I said.

"I saw you playing with little Kris over there."

"Yeah, he's a cutie. Do you mind if I ask what happened to his mother?"

"Oh, she died during childbirth. It was a high-risk pregnancy. I'm not sure exactly what happened, but she had health issues before she got pregnant. High blood pressure, I think."

"So sad! He never got to meet his mom. And his father never remarried?"

"Look at you, out on the prowl. I knew you'd like him."

"I'm not out on the prowl, exactly, and yes, I did find him attractive. I wouldn't mind talking to him some more."

"You'll get your chance. He'll probably stay until midnight so long as the little one stays asleep."

I was on the lookout for Lance the rest of the evening, but he knew so many people at the party. Everyone kept pulling him away to talk. He was a social butterfly and I was more of a wallflower. We enjoyed a few stolen glances at each other across the room, but never got a chance to talk again. It was nearly midnight. My eyes were heavy and I knew I had to get home soon. I was used to going to bed early in the evenings and this was late for me.

I gathered my purse and coat and headed into the party room where the countdown had begun. I was looking for Bonnie to say good-bye. "Ten, nine, eight," everyone chimed in together. "Seven, six, five…" I felt a hand on my shoulder. "Four, three, two…" I swiveled my head around to see who it was. "One. Happy New Year!" I felt a warm, sweet kiss on lips and strong arms wrapped around my waist. It was Lance. He was a good kisser.

He whispered in my ear, "Happy New Year. I don't even know your name."

"Chelsey," I said. "That was a nice surprise."

"I'm Kris," he said.

"Kris? I thought that was your son's name."

"It is. He's a junior."

"I thought I heard Bonnie call you 'Lance' earlier this evening."

"Yeah, she calls me Sir Lancelot, it's a little nickname she's been calling me for years. High school play."

Then it dawned on me. I had just kissed Kristof Beck, the owner of Bratz.

"It's nice to meet you," I said.

"It's nice to meet you too."

He leaned in and gave me another soft, gentle kiss on the lips.

"Are you leaving?" he asked. He must have noticed my coat and purse in hand.

"Yes, it's late for me."

"I'd love to take you out sometime."

"I'd like that," I said.

It was then I knew what I wanted to do with my life…at least for a little while.

Made in the USA
Charleston, SC
13 April 2013